The W

Magnificent Grace

by

Skelton Yawngrave

To Mira

Thank you! ☺ ☺

Hope you like this story.

Skelton

Yawngrave

March 2020

DANGER!

This copy of *Magnificent Grace* has been preserved for research purposes only. Naturally, the other copies have been deleted or burnt.

If you are an Ordinary child and you have found this book, give it to the nearest adult in authority, and explain how you came by this forbidden material.

If you are a Normal thief, understand that we will find you. The witch Grace Brown and the traitor Skelton Yawngrave cannot protect you forever.

Ordinary is as Ordinary does!

Ann Bland
Chief Executive and Chairperson
Ordinary People's Party

Ordinary, adjective
1. With no special or distinctive features, normal.
Oxford English Dictionary

Normal, adjective
1. Ordinary or usual, the same as would be expected.
Cambridge English Dictionary

Part I

Grace and The Grey Menace

Chapter 1

Ribs a-go-go

It was a week before Halloween, but this year there would be no trick-or-treating.

On their way to the *Ribs a-go-go* restaurant, the Brown family drove past two Normal men hurrying along the pavement. The men wore their top hats, bow ties, purple suits and flowery waistcoats with pride. Their clothes stood out among the drab hoodies, fleeces and coats of the Ordinary people on the street. These perfectly Normal men looked slim as skeletons. They had thin gleaming faces and a brisk, elbowy way of walking. One of them twirled a silver-tipped cane.

'Why do they have to dress like that?' said Mrs Brown to her husband who was driving. She turned to scowl at Grace and Molly, in the back seats, in case they were still looking at the men.

Keeping his eyes on the road, Mr Brown said nothing.

When she had a chance, Grace, who was the older girl, opened her tiny turquoise notebook to record some observations in her meticulous writing.

Here's what she wrote.

Observations: THE BIG PARENT CHANGE day 13

1. *Parents still acting weirdly.*
2. *Forced to wear the same clothes as Molly again.*
3. *Mum is OBSESSED with grey clothes.*
4. *Mum is still being horrible about Normal people.*

Before she hid her notebook in her pocket, she added one more item:

5. *Dad seems angry all the time. Why?*

Minutes later, the family were being shown to one of the snug booths that lined the walls of the *Ribs a-go-go*. Molly and Mrs Brown slid in first, facing each other. Then Grace sat next to her sister, opposite her father. It was busy. All the booths were full, and only one table near them was empty. Nearby, the open kitchen was a clamour of sizzles, clangs and bustling cries.

Catching the eye of a busy waiter, Mrs Brown immediately ordered sticky barbeque ribs and fries for the whole family. As the waiter hurried off, however, a curious hush fell in the restaurant.

Everyone had stopped to stare. The skeleton men they had noticed earlier were now in *Ribs-a-go-go*. Waiting to be seated, they politely touched the brims of their top hats. The taller of the two squeaked his thumb on the silver knob of his walking stick. He smiled, showing lots of teeth. Eventually the youngest of the waiters was sent to speak to them.

Gradually, talk began again. People gnawed at ribs, licked sauce from their fingers and dug at their teeth with toothpicks. Everyone, however, was still aware of the two well-dressed gentlemen being led across the room, and some darted spiteful sideways glances at them. Grace cringed. They were shown the last free table, which was right next to the Brown family's booth. It was only a matter of time before her mother said something horrible.

To distract herself, Grace took out a magnifying glass from her pocket to observe a tiny object she noticed near her knife. Grace saw it was the squished head of a dead fly with colourful compound eyes. Examining this was far better than looking at her mother.

As he sat down, the man with the silver-tipped cane nodded politely in their direction. Mr and Mrs Brown pretended they had not seen him. Grace saw him grin eagerly as he and his friend were handed scruffy *Normals Only* menus by a waiter.

'Well, that's ruined it,' muttered Mrs Brown to her husband, 'I can't bear to watch people like *that* eating.'

Mr Brown said nothing.

Although Grace continued to study the insect's head, she was secretly listening to the thin men's penetrating voices.

'What sort of ribs do you favour Skelton, old stick?' asked one.

'Well, they have such a variety at *Ribs a go-go*, Bonaparte.'

'Indeed they do,' said the one called Bonaparte.

From the corner of her eye, Grace watched his knobbly finger travelling down the Normal menu. 'Anaconda ribs!' he said. 'Anacondas must have hundreds of ribs.'

'Interesting,' replied Skelton. 'But today I have a taste for octopus ribs.'

'Octopuses don't have ribs.'

It took the men a few moments to realise that it was Grace who had spoken.

The one called Skelton answered politely. 'Of course you are right, young lady, they are more chewy than bony now I come to think of it.'

'Octopuses are invertebrates,' Grace said, 'they don't have a backbone, so they can't have ribs.'

'You're a brainy girl,' Skelton said, flashing his long teeth at her.

'Yes I am,' said Grace, who was both brainy and factual.

'My name is Skelton Kirkley Elvis Lionel Lupus Yawngrave III,' the skeleton man said, smiling at her. 'My name, of course, is a Normal name. And my companion, my oldest friend, is Bonaparte Owen Navicular Eduardo Yarpgrater.'

'They are both excellent Normal names,' said Grace with equal politeness. 'My name is Grace Brown.'

'That's a good, wholesome, Ordinary name,' said Skelton thoughtfully, 'but it could be a bit longer.'

'Perhaps it will expand as she ages,' said Bonaparte.

Grace glanced at her magnifying glass.

'Maybe it will,' she said. 'I'd like to be called Grace "The Mighty Microscope" Brown, because I want to be famous for using magnification to make scientific discoveries and detailed observations.'

Skelton smiled again. 'Very scientific of—'

'Grace!' her mother yelped, her mushroom grey nails digging into the palms of her hands. 'I've told you before! You are not to talk to strangers. Especially to *Normals*,' she said, glancing at Skelton and Bonaparte.

Grace felt her face grow hot, but her mother had not finished.

'And stop going on about that precious microscope. When you grow up you are going to be a model and wear fashionable clothes. Now eat!'

Pocketing her magnifying glass, Grace dutifully began to nibble at the sweet and meaty ribs. Her attention, however, was still on the two men who had removed their jackets and were carefully rolling up their shirtsleeves. Their arms were slim and white.

Soon Skelton and Bonaparte were chomping the tough meat from dozens of curly anaconda bones, their jaws creaking with effort. Grace noticed how quickly they ate, wolfing twenty or thirty ribs in the time it took her to eat one or two.

'Whew,' said Bonaparte, breaking the silence as he put down his ninety-seventh snake rib and rested his elbows on the table. Skelton groaned in reply. His own plate was also a precarious tower of bones.

Something knocked Grace's knee. Her little sister Molly was squeezing out from under the table.

Grace's mother had not noticed. She was talking about finding a new job, and how expensive eating out was. Molly, her face decorated with barbecue sauce, darted happily towards the skeleton men. She stood for a moment, smiling up inquisitively at Bonaparte. Suddenly she bit his arm quite hard.

Bonaparte rocketed from his seat. 'The *rudeness*!' Everyone was staring again.

'Sorry,' said Molly in a small voice. 'I got mixed up.'

'Leave her alone!' Mrs Brown screamed. 'Bob, *do* something!'

Grace's father leapt up to seize Bonaparte by his thin neck. The piles of curly bones toppled onto the floor. Meanwhile, Mrs Brown scooped Molly into her arms as if she were in terrible danger. Grace frozenly watched her father grapple with the thin man.

'Help!' Bonaparte managed to choke out.

'Let him go! I demand it!' Skelton said, poking Mr Brown with a long finger.

At last Grace's father came to his senses, and appeared a little ashamed as he released the other man's neck. Bonaparte doubled over, gasping for breath. Everyone in the restaurant began talking at once.

The manager arrived. Grace observed beads of sweat on his forehead.

'I don't want any of your Normal trouble,' he said to the two smart gentlemen. 'I try to be fair, but you people just don't help yourselves, do you? Pay up and get out.'

'But...' began Bonaparte, rubbing his neck.

Skelton shook his head in warning at Bonaparte. Quickly, they rolled down their shirtsleeves, put in their cufflinks and slid their arms into their jackets.

'Here's your money,' Skelton said to the manager, handing him a wad of wrinkled notes. 'But I'll have you know we're law-abiding citizens. We did nothing wrong.'

'Just go,' the manager said, snatching their money without counting it.

Retrieving their top hats from under their seats, the elegant men walked to the exit with injured dignity.

'What else can you expect from Normals?' Mrs Brown said loudly. A mutter of agreement passed from table to table. 'I agree with Mrs Bland!' she added.

But Grace had other ideas. Before her mother could stop her, she jumped from her seat and ran out of the restaurant.

Outside, Bonaparte was adjusting his collar as Skelton peered at him in concern. Suddenly someone was pulling at Bonaparte's jacket sleeve. It was Grace.

'What *now*?' he snapped.

'I'm sorry, Mr Bonaparte. Molly didn't mean any rudeness.'

'I know,' said Bonaparte. 'Biting poor old Bonaparte was just a mistake. The strangling, however, was done on purpose.'

'Yes,' Skelton said. 'Trouble follows us these days. But, it is good to know that there are some Ordinary folks with excellent manners and kind natures. Good luck with your microscoping, Grace Brown.'

'That's not a proper word,' said Bonaparte.

'She knows what I mean,' Skelton said. 'Don't you, Grace?'

With that, the thin men walked off.

Grace turned to go back inside. She was in trouble.

Chapter 2

All about Grace

'Such style, Grace,' sighed Mrs Brown. 'Just *look* at her suit.' She stopped tidying the kitchen to admire the iron grey suit that the famous Mrs Bland was wearing on breakfast television. It was the first time she had spoken to Grace since the argument in *Ribs a-go-go* two days ago.

'Hmm,' Grace answered, chomping the last bit of her buttered toast.

'Grey is this year's black, Grace. So stylish and understated,' continued her mother dreamily. 'When you are on the catwalk perhaps you'll wear clothes like Mrs Bland.'

'I don't want to become a model,' said Grace putting her plate into the dishwasher, 'and I hate grey.'

'We'll see,' said her mother, smoothing down her skirt. She was dressed in work clothes, but she had no shoes on her feet. 'You're too young to know what's best.'

Grace pulled a face.

'Don't! How can you shine in photographs if you keep twisting your face? And I've told you before to stop rolling your eyes.' Her mother irritably turned off the TV.

'Mum, why don't you listen to me? I want to work in biological sciences. I like insects, and pond life like cyclopes, daphnia and planarian worms,' she said, packing a book about butterflies into her school bag. 'And dragonflies! Dragonflies are so beautiful.'

'Pond life? What's wrong with you?' Worms aren't interesting, Grace. Worms aren't Ordinary for a pretty little girl like you. Mrs Bland wants people to live Ordinary lives, and she's quite right. That's what I want for you, Grace. I want to see you modelling a charcoal dress in a catalogue one day. I'd be so happy.'

'Mum I don't *want* to. Why should I? You're not a model. You used to work in an office.'

'I did, didn't I?' Grace's mother said sourly. She had lost her job a few weeks before, and was still searching for another one. She slammed the dishwasher door angrily. 'So you think you're too good to be a model?'

'Mum! It's just that I'm not particularly interested in clothes,' said Grace. 'They're boring.'

'Bored by fashion?' her mother interrupted. 'Bored? What kind of a girl are you? You're eleven now. Mrs Bland would say that Ordinary girls should focus on appropriate opportunities. Ogling those disgusting wrigglers under a microscope isn't Ordinary!'

Grace noted how her mother clenched her fingers *and* her toes in irritation.

'I can't believe your father gave you that microscope. After all, we're a completely Ordinary family... One hundred per cent Ordinary.' An anxious expression passed over her face. 'Perhaps we should recycle that thing and have it made into something useful, like spoons or stud earrings. Mrs Bland would agree, I'm sure.'

Luckily for Grace, Molly chose that moment to run into the kitchen.

'Molly, have you brushed your teeth properly?' her mother asked.

'Yes, every single one,' said Molly. 'What is Mrs Bland?'

'I've already told you this. Mrs Bland is a person, Molly. I hope you grow up just like her. She is leader of the Ordinary People's Party; our party.'

'Balloons?' said Molly.

'A *political* party. I have explained this to you before.'

'She's nasty,' said Grace, before she could stop herself.

'That's enough, Grace!' Mrs Brown said, grabbing a packet of cornflakes and slamming a cupboard door. 'I've had more than enough from you lately. Talking to those two *things* in the restaurant the other night... I've told you so many times! You *don't* talk to Normals. Not now Mrs Bland's almost in power.'

'Is that why you got dad to strangle Mr Bonaparte?' said Grace.

'Bonaparte, was it? The names these people give themselves! No, your father was protecting Molly from that *monster*.'

'They are not monsters,' said Grace, angrily. 'They didn't do any harm, and Molly started it—'

'No harm? No harm?' Grace's mother was suddenly furious, and waving an eggy spoon in the air. 'Go to your room this minute! I've had enough.'

'But I have to go to school!' Grace grabbed her bag defiantly.

'School? It just makes you worse, filling your head with nonsense. You don't need to know about poems or planets or plant life or any other of those things. All you'll need to know is how to wear a nice slate grey dress and look pretty in it.'

'But I should go to school by law,' muttered Grace.

'I'm the law in this house. And if I find you squinting at specimens when I come up, that microscope is history.'

'Biology, *actually*,' yelled Grace, stamping upstairs to her bedroom.

'You come back here!' her mother shouted. Grace turned and slowly came downstairs. Her mother was waiting with her hand out. 'Phone,' she said. 'Two days.'

Once in her room, Grace immediately hid her microscope under her desk, in case her mother decided to confiscate that too. Then she sat cross-legged on the bed, flipping through the pages of her tiny turquoise notebook. Since *The Big Parent Change* had started, one name appeared on every page: Mrs Bland.

Grace's parents used to be proud of their elder daughter's intelligence. In the last few weeks, however, everything had changed. Her mother's fixation with grey clothes was just one sign of her infatuation with Mrs Bland. When the politician began to say abusive things about Normal people, Mrs Brown began to ignore her Normal friends, passing them in the street and not answering their phone calls.

Grace realised she needed a plan. She needed a stupendous stratagem, an eye-popping inspiration to make Mrs Bland look stupid; a thunderously good theory to make everyone see that she should be tied to a giant boulder and catapulted to the moon.

I wonder, she thought, *if anyone else is thinking the same thing as me? I wonder if—*

Without knocking, her mother barged into her bedroom, and plonked a tin of paint on the desk. Grace saw the name of the colour was *London Pavement*.

'Instead of sulking on your bed, you can paint this wall,' she pointed to the wall opposite Grace's bed. Quickly, she returned with a paint roller, a tray and some brushes. Immediately she pulled away a poster of the life cycle of a frog.

'Nasty tadpoles! And this silly buttercup colour underneath is a bad influence. It is unusual, Grace. It has to go.'

'But this is grey, Mum,' Grace said picking up the heavy tin, 'I don't like grey.'

'You do now! It is a wonderfully fashionable and Ordinary colour. Help me spread this sheet on the floor so you can paint this wall instead of wasting your time at school.'

For the next hour Grace's paint roller went: *grey, grey, grey* and covered the sunshine like a cloud.

I hate this, thought Grace, wiping at the drab paint that was getting on her hands.

Later, her mother popped her head around the door.

'So much better! And I've just had a thought,' she said, smiling sweetly. 'Why don't we stop calling you *Grace*, and start calling you *Grey* instead?'

Crying, as everyone knows, is exhausting. When Grace woke up it was getting dark.

It seemed her father had arrived home unusually early. Lying dejectedly on her bed, Grace heard her mother emit a squeal of excitement downstairs. Moments later, her parents burst excitedly into her room.

'Wake up Grace! We have exciting news,' said her father. It was the first time he had spoken in days. He seemed pleased with himself.

'Grey,' said her mother. 'We've agreed that Grey should be her new name. Lovely, isn't it?'

'Grey.' Her father narrowed his eyes thoughtfully. 'Yes, it suits her.'

'No it doesn't!' said Grace. 'That's not my name!'

'Anyway, *Grey*, your father is trying to tell you that we have received a last-minute invitation to a fundraising ball.'

'What's a fundraising ball?' asked Grace.

'It's a social gathering to raise money for a good cause.'

Grace still did not understand.

'It's for Mrs Bland's political party, the O.P.P.' her mother continued impatiently, 'The Ordinary People's Party. It will be wonderful! I am so proud that our family was invited. You and Molly must come too. We must hurry! The ball is tonight, Grey. Tonight! We all must be smart of course. Bob, you can wear your nice suit, and I will wear my best mouse grey dress. The children will wear new lovely French grey outfits. It's a great honour for our family.'

'I don't want to go,' said Grace.

'You do what you're told,' said her father. 'Don't you want to see Mrs Bland? She's famous.'

Perhaps, thought Grace, *I can make some observations about Mrs Bland.*

'Okay,' she said aloud.

'Good,' her father said. He smiled at her for the first time in days. 'Now scrub that paint off your hands, grab your dress and hurry!'

Chapter 3

The Grey Ball

Both girls' hair was painfully plaited into pigtails, and they had been forced to wear grey clothes. Grace's father wore a sombre suit, which made him look old. Mrs Brown wore a skirt and jacket just like Mrs Bland.

'Come on Molly, and you, Grace... *Grey*,' Mrs Brown corrected herself.

'Into the car,' said Mr Brown.

It was six-thirty in the evening, and it was already dark. The streets they drove through were unusually crowded. Men stood in watchful clumps of threes and fours, as if waiting for some kind of trouble.

'Who are those men?' asked Grace.

'They're from the Ordinary People's Party,' said Grace's mother. 'They support Mrs Bland.'

The town hall, when they arrived, was decked out in flags with the silver letters O.P.P. on them. A giant poster of Mrs Bland's face loomed above the entrance.

Grace remembered her mission. She was here to observe Mrs Bland and the Ordinary People's Party. As they neared the entrance, a man in grey stopped a woman who was queuing just in front of them.

'Not you,' he said.

'I'm sorry?' The woman was surprised and embarrassed.

'I can't let you in wearing *that* colour. Don't you know anything? Mrs Bland says red's *not Ordinary*, you should know that.'

Grace had been ordered to leave her magnifying glass at home, and her mother was still keeping her phone as punishment. She had, however, managed to smuggle her tiny turquoise notebook and a small pink pen in her pocket. Hastily she scribbled, *Observation 1 – Mrs Bland hates colourful dresses.*

They were shown to a large round table. Two grey-clothed families had arrived before them. Soon all the adults were talking. Grace tried listening to the music produced by a band of silver-haired men on the stage. One boring tune slurred into the next.

Observation 2 – Mrs Bland likes horrible music. Grace rested the notebook on her lap under the table as she wrote. The adults were so involved in telling each other how Ordinary they were that none of them paid her any attention until her mother said, 'Of course, my daughter Grey hopes to go into modelling and become a fashion influencer.'

'Grey? What a perfect name,' said one of the women enviously, clearly wishing she had named her daughter Grey too.

At the table were two other girls with grey nail polish. They had eyed Grace mockingly when her mother had been boasting. Next to Grace was a boy called Peter, who had ignored her till now.

'First time?' he asked.

'Yes,' said Grace.

'This is my third. Dad says they're letting anyone in now.' His voice was snooty. 'Everyone goes crazy when she speaks. That's if you're old enough to really *get* her, that is.'

'Why do you like Mrs Bland so much?' Grace asked.

'Because the trouble with this country is that there are too many stinking Normals, and my parents think Mrs Bland's going to do something about it.'

'What do *you* think?' asked Grace.

'The same as Mrs Bland, of course. She does the thinking,' said Peter. 'All we have to do is agree with her.'

Observation 3 — Mrs Bland hates anyone thinking for themselves.

Waiters arrived with chicken, dollops of watery mashed potato, some white bread and mould-green peas.

'Mmm,' said Grace's mum, 'nice Ordinary food. Eat up girls,' she said to Grace and Molly.

Observation 4 – Mrs Bland likes tasteless food, Grace wrote, sipping the flat tap water in her glass.

Observation 5 – Mrs Bland doesn't like bubbles.

Now there seemed to be hundreds of supporters in the hall. One or two couples started woodenly circling the dance floor, their feet sliding mechanically to the dreary music.

Observation 6 – Mrs Bland hates dancing.

The music changed, and became more strident. A recording of a massed choir blasted from speakers. The song the choir sang went something like this:

> *'Ordinary People like you and me*
> *are very proud to be Ordinary*
> *so happy to be Ordinary*
> *Ordinary People like you and meeeee...*
> *We love our Ordinary country...*
> *and the good old O.P.P.*
> *Men and women like you and meeeee...*
> *boys and girls like you and meeeee...*
> *in the good old O.P.P!'*

A man standing on the platform began clapping his hands as hard as he could. Almost at once, everyone else was applauding too.

There she was!

Mrs Bland was welcomed like a pop star. All around the room men and women stood up, cheering. She walked to the centre of the stage and waved regally.

'Stand up!' Grace's mother hissed at her older daughter.

The man on the stage raised a pudgy hand. Eventually the clapping stopped.

'It is my honour to introduce our leader and inspiration! The Queen of the O.P.P! Mrs Ann Bland!'

Mrs Bland smiled dazzlingly into the lenses of nearby cameras. There were more cheers from the audience, and she waited graciously till the applause came to a stop.

'What a pleasure to see so many honest, Ordinary people gathered in one place,' she began. 'And I want to tell you one thing. If anyone criticises you for being proudly Ordinary, tell them this. Ordinary people are the backbone of this country. Ordinary people made this country great.'

Thunderous applause followed. Everyone, except Grace, was clapping. She had just noticed that Mrs Bland wore enormous diamonds in her ears. They glittered splendidly in the stage lights. Anyone else,

Grace thought, who had worn huge jewels would have been turned away at the door, just like the woman with the red dress.

Observation 7 – Mrs Bland likes diamonds, but doesn't want anyone else to wear them.

'But my friends,' Mrs Bland continued, 'our Ordinary way of life is being threatened. And we all know who is doing that, don't we?'

'Yes we do!' several in the crowd shouted.

'What threatens us, my dear friends, is the *unusual.*' She made the word sound repulsive. 'It is the *unusual* inhabitants of this country.'

'Normals!' a woman shouted. Grace realised, with horror, that her mother had called out as she gazed lovingly at Mrs Bland.

'I am not saying we should kill unusual people. I'm saying that they should go away to where their kind came from. All the O.P.P. demands is that we have a country that is free and safe for Ordinary people.'

Observation 8 – Grace wrote in her notebook, *Mrs Bland is a dangerous lunatic who should be strapped to a giant boulder and catapulted to the moon.*

'I am an Ordinary person,' said Mrs Bland sounding tremendously sincere. 'And I want our iron grey flags to flutter over Parliament. I want the royal family to wear grey and answer to Ordinary folks. I want to make it illegal to be *unusual*. I can tell you now that I have ordered a letter to be sent to every Normal house in the country. It will tell them that Halloween has been banned!'

More uproarious support, hooting and clapping, rose in the room.

'No longer will Ordinary citizens of this country tolerate freaks. We will not tolerate witchcraft. It is time we just said no to Halloween. It is *unusual*. It is depraved. It is wrong! Wrong! Wrong!'

More tremendous applause followed. The speech was over.

Mrs Bland left the platform and began to walk among the crowd, shaking her admirer's hands. Nervously, Grace saw she was now approaching their table. Photographers scurried behind her.

Peter, still clapping, turned to Grace. 'This is where they take the photos. Last time, I was photographed with her!'

Tonight, however, Mrs Bland ignored Peter, despite how he strained towards her. Instead she positioned herself between Grace and Molly. The girls were suddenly blinded by camera flashes.

'And what have we here?' said Mrs Bland, seizing the tiny turquoise notebook from Grace. More cameras flashed. She leant down and whispered behind her hand.

'Are you a sneaking little reporter?' she asked, pretending to the cameras that she was sharing a joke with a young supporter.

Grace gulped. Something in Mrs Bland's eyes, a green flicker, was horribly piercing.

'No,' she whispered.

Mrs Bland cleared her throat, and the laugher quickly died away.

'This darling child,' she said. 'What is your name, dear?'

'Grey, Mrs Bland,' said her mother quickly.

'Grey? What a lovely name. How Ordinary.'

Mrs Brown glowed with pride.

Idly Mrs Bland toyed with Grace's notebook. It fell open.

'Let me see,' said Mrs Bland. 'Biology field trip to Mrs Bland Land,' she said, reading aloud. 'How funny, dear. With any luck the whole of this country will soon be Mrs Bland Land.'

More laughter, and scattered clapping. The whirring click of cameras.

Mrs Bland continued, 'Observation 1 – Mrs Bland hates colourful clothes.' And, more quietly, 'Observation 2 – Mrs Bland likes horrible music.'

The room hushed as Mrs Bland read the rest of the list in silence.

'Apparently,' Mrs Bland said, 'I am a dangerous lunatic who should be strapped to a giant boulder and catapulted to the *moon*!'

A gasp. Grace's mother hid her face in her hands. One or two people cried out 'No!' or 'Shame!' Several booed.

Mrs Bland fixed Grace with a paralysing stare. Even the photographers stopped. Everyone was waiting to see how she would deal with this impertinent child.

'Does anyone think this girl is funny?' asked Mrs Bland.

'No!' said several people loudly.

'This *list* is clearly not the work of an O.P.P. member. Whose child is this?' she demanded, her eyes not leaving Grace.

'Mine, Mrs Bland,' Grace's mother stammered.

Now Mrs Bland's eyes fixed on Mrs Brown. 'I expect you've tried quite hard with this girl, haven't you?' she said quietly.

'Yes... Yes I have,' said Grace's mother. 'But she can be very difficult, can't she, Bob?' She glanced urgently at her husband.

'Yes,' said Grace's father dully, 'difficult.'

'So I can see,' said Mrs Bland. She seized Grace's arm, digging her long nails into the girl's skin.

Grace winced.

'But this child is in luck,' said the politician sounding beautiful again, 'for she can be cured. The Ordinary People's Party has a school for children who find it hard to be Ordinary. For we must not blame our children. They have grown up in a world crawling with *unusual* individuals. Some children, like Grey' – here Mrs Bland pressed her nails even harder into Grace's arm –'will need to be corrected.'

Grace's mother nodded vigorously at her leader.

'My own boys attend Charcoal House, so I can be sure they receive the most Ordinary education possible. I am willing to offer this Grey girl the opportunity to come to Charcoal House where she will be taught some discipline in the Ordinary way. Mr and Mrs...?'

'Brown,' said Grace's mother.

'Mrs Brown,' said Mrs Bland soothingly. 'Would you like me to give your child the opportunity of a lifetime, and the chance to become perfectly Ordinary?'

Grace looked pleadingly at her parents.

'Well, Mrs Bland,' said Mrs Brown, 'I've always said I want Grey to grow up just like you.'

'Just like me?' Mrs Bland said, her eyes flashing at Grace.

'Please, Mum... I don't want to!' said Grace, finding her voice at last.

Her mother, however, was almost in tears of gratitude.

'Mrs Bland, I'd be honoured if you would take Grey to Charcoal House. All we want is for her to grow up to be an Ordinary citizen that we can be proud of.'

Grace tried to speak again, but her tongue had become a stone. Her eyes grew round with fear.

'Well said, Mrs Brown!' crowed Mrs Bland. 'A round of applause!'

Everyone clapped.

'Mum,' gasped Grace. Her mother's eyes were shining and hard.

'You see?' Mrs Bland said. 'This is the kind of support the Ordinary People's Party provides for Ordinary families.'

Grace was astonished. How could her mother just give her away?

'Nick! Rick! Dick!' called Mrs Bland.

From behind the stage curtain, the three sons of Mrs Bland emerged to a smattering of applause. They were dressed like little businessmen, in slate-grey suits. Nick, the eldest, was almost thirteen. At eight, Dick was the youngest. Rick, the middle brother, appeared to be the same age as Grace. All three had close-cropped hair and forgettable faces. Rick was a little different. He had metal braces on his teeth, and was more hunched and burly than his brothers.

'To the car please, boys,' Mrs Bland said.

The three brothers led a stunned Grace away from the table. She turned back once to see her parents' faces glowing with pride, but Molly was starting to cry.

Once no one could see them, the boys grew rougher. They dragged Grace down a flight of stairs, pushing her and pinning her arms to her sides.

'Let me go!' Grace struggled desperately at a door marked FIRE EXIT. But it was three against one. The two older brothers on each side, the youngest one yanking her plaits from behind. The middle brother seemed especially strong.

'Help!' she shouted. 'Help!'

No one came.

'Help me, I'm so afraid,' mocked the eldest boy in a pathetic voice.

They shoved her through another door and out across a concrete drive towards a shiny black limousine. The car even had black windows.

Still Grace wriggled and punched. For a split second she almost broke free. The street was just a sprint away. A man, Mrs Bland's driver, sprang from the car. He was talking on a mobile phone, but with one arm he casually thrust her through an open rear door. The boys piled in after her.

Frantic, Grace slid across the seat to the other door, but it gave a heavy clunk

Trapped.

The youngest boy punched her shoulder.

'You idiot. Stop it!' Grace yelled.

This time the boys backed off.

Fury stung her eyes. The brothers nudged one another, and the youngest one laughed.

It was not the boys who were making her cry, though. It was far worse. It seemed her mother could not wait to be rid of her. Had her mother stopped loving her?

Grace banged her head against the headrest, forcing herself to stop crying in front of these stupid boys.

As usual, she started to make observations. The car was huge; another four children could have fitted in beside them. It smelt of leather and air freshener, and the seats were soft. It even had even lamps with lampshades. Grace could see out of the smoked black glass, but she knew nobody outside could see her.

The boys were now completely ignoring her. They were all gaming.

'Where are you taking me?' she asked.

'Mother said not to talk to you,' said Dick, the youngest, pulling out an earphone but still shooting at coloured targets and turning them to ash, 'so we're not going to.'

'Suit yourselves,' said Grace.

There were explosions all over Dick's screen. Watching, despite herself, Grace slowly realised that all the targets he was killing were Normal.

Chapter 4

Charcoal House

Mrs Bland stepped briskly into the back of the car. Grace, who had leant forward, was again pushed firmly into her seat. Another man sat in the front next to the driver. Almost silently, a glass screen rose up between the two men and the passengers. Having been given away by her mother, Grace was now sealed in the back of the car with Mrs Bland and her sons.

The limousine slid like a gleaming black shark into the shoals of night-time traffic. As everyone ignored her, Grace ignored them too. She gazed through the car window, and soon she no longer recognised the streets.

Mrs Bland was staring at her. 'For some reason I seem to know your face. Have you been to one of our balls before?' she asked.

'Nope,' Grace said eventually.

Mrs Bland had moved her hand a few inches towards Grace, almost as if she were going to touch her. But instead, her mouth grimaced. 'You will pay for your *unusual* insolence. You do understand that, don't you?'

She did not wait for an answer. Instead she opened her handbag. Grace's notebook lay inside, next to a glittering phial of expensive perfume. She removed the book with distaste, and began to flick through it, studying drawings of a mosquito Grace had made using her microscope. There were four pages where she had been practising her signature using lots of flamboyant flourishes. Mrs Bland saw her name was *Grace* Brown, not Grey Brown.

'Think a lot of yourself, don't you?' she said.

Next she found a story Grace had begun to write. It was about Mr Bonaparte and Mr Yawngrave. Grace squirmed with embarrassment. This was private.

'How do you know Skelton Yawngrave?' Mrs Bland's voice was sharp.

Grace answered the question with a question. 'Why have you kidnapped me?'

Mrs Bland's plump lips thinned. Her cold eyes blazed at Grace. 'I am going to ask you a question, and I want you to think hard before you answer me, Grace Brown,' she said. 'Do you love your parents?'

'Yes,' said Grace, trying to recall them before *THE BIG PARENT CHANGE*, 'of course I do.'

'But remember how easily your parents gave you away to me. Do you imagine they love you as much as you love them?'

'Yes, they do—' Grace began.

'I wouldn't be so certain. Think! They gave you to me in a second, just because I asked them to,' said Mrs Bland. 'You know what? I'm not even sure they can be your real parents.'

Grace wanted to shout, *they are my real parents*. Mrs Bland's face was smiling. Why was she being so cruel? The woman had only known her for a few minutes, but she understood how to hurt her already.

'Your problem, Grey or Grace or whatever you call yourself, is that you are not Ordinary enough,' Mrs Bland continued. 'You have a fixation with so-called Normal people,' she said, tapping irritably with a talon-like nail at Grace's notebook. 'And I can tell that you think you're better than your Ordinary family, don't you?'

'I don't want to be your kind of Ordinary,' said Grace, 'if it means pretending to be stupid and hating Normal people. People are people. It doesn't matter if they are Normal or Ordinary.'

Anger was radiating from Mrs Bland.

'Do you know anything at all, you wretched girl? *Normals* are full of hate. They dabble in magic to undermine us. Their ridiculous beliefs and disgusting customs threaten decent people who are trying to lead Ordinary lives. Their flamboyance and imagination are really just excuses to tell lies. They are not proper people, you stupid girl. Some of these so called Normal *people*, are actually talking animals, and… Vampires and skeletons and the like. They don't belong in this world, there is nothing natural about them.'

'But some of my friends are Normal, and Mum and Dad's friends—'

'Your parents have Normal friends?' Mrs Bland flared dangerously.

'They used to have lots of them,' said Grace sadly. 'But since they started listening to you—'

'They came to their senses,' said Mrs Bland, clenching her fist. 'It's as I suspected. You're a disobedient little fool rebelling against her parents. No wonder they wanted to get rid of you.'

'Well you're worse than a fool!' Grace shouted, her voice choking. 'You pretend to be a weird kind of Ordinary person who only wears grey and eats tasteless food. But this car isn't Ordinary, your diamonds aren't either. And my Mum—'

'What a creature you are,' said Mrs Bland, with a laugh like cracking ice. Glancing at her sons who were lost in their games, she leant towards Grace. 'But you are quite right,' she whispered, 'I am not Ordinary at all. I am extraordinary. An extraordinary person! I am not like those bleating sheep in that dingy town hall. I am Mrs Bland and you would be a fool to underestimate me.'

'What happens if I tell people that you think you are better than them?' asked Grace.

Mrs Bland laughed again. 'Oh my dear, that won't be an issue. For you won't remember this! You are going to be changed. Charcoal House will grind away your *unusual* edges, and smooth you into being properly Ordinary. Now, of course, you are no more than a disturbed child, but in a few years you might become a useful party worker. And then you will love me, Grace, just wait and see. You'll love me more than your ridiculous mother.'

'But—' began Grace.

'Stop talking!' Mrs Bland hissed. She flashed out her hand, and slapped Grace hard in the face.

Stunned, her cheek stinging, Grace pretended to watch the other cars on the motorway. Mrs Bland, she decided, would be her enemy as long as she lived.

It was late. The car had rocked Grace to sleep, even though she did not feel safe. Waking up and realising she was still in Mrs Bland's car was depressing. She felt for her phone and remembered that her mother had confiscated it. Nor was her shocking-pink watch on her wrist because her mother had said it was *not Ordinary enough*.

Through half-closed eyes, Grace observed Mrs Bland, who was still facing her, but working on a blade thin laptop computer. Two of the boys had fallen asleep, but Rick was awake. He was listening to headphones, and absentmindedly worrying at his braces with his fingers.

Suddenly, Mrs Bland's patience snapped. She tore the headphones from Rick's ears. 'I've told you a million times!'

The boy flinched. 'I apologise,' he stammered, jerking his finger guiltily from his mouth. His shoulders hunched even more.

The limousine left the motorway to squeeze into narrow country lanes. On either side was farmland and woods, and once in a while they drove through a village, where teenagers waiting at a bus stop stared as the mysterious, black-windowed car swept by.

The car slowed, driving through woodland. The headlights made a bright tunnel of the overhanging branches, and lit up the falling leaves. As they emerged from the trees, a huge, slab-like building came into view. The grounds were surrounded by a high barbed-wire fence. As their limousine approached, metal gates automatically opened to let them in.

Grace heard the tyres crunching on gravel before the driver stopped the limousine outside the building's entrance. The other man stepped smartly out to open the passenger door.

The middle brother, Rick, shook Nick and Dick awake. The three boys stepped sleepily into the cold, and walked towards the building. Mrs Bland was having a phone conversation, which seemed to be about Halloween.

'Thank you Prime Minister and goodnight,' she said, her face flushed with triumph.

She turned to Grace, still smiling. 'Welcome to Charcoal House.'

They were outside a windowed reception area, through which Grace could glimpse a grim, paved courtyard. The rest of the building was forbidding. It had flat featureless walls, dotted with a few tiny windows. It had been built to keep secrets, Grace decided. The idea of leaving the car to go into this concrete fortress scared her.

'The sooner you enter, the sooner you'll learn how to like it,' said Mrs Bland. If I can force the Government to stamp out Halloween, trick-or-treating and all that nonsense, I can make *you*, a mere child, do anything I want. Now hurry!'

Grace climbed reluctantly from the car, shivering in the thin clothes her mother had made her wear to the Grey Ball.

'Mrs Bland strode into the concrete building, and Grace trotted behind her to keep up.

They entered a cheerless reception area. Mrs Bland's portrait hung above the desk, which was manned by two security guards in uniforms. They stood up smartly. Behind them, Grace observed a single tree in the darkness of the courtyard.

Another man in a business suit appeared from an office to the side of the desk. The soles of his shoes tapped metallically on the stone floor.

'Another one, Madam?' he asked.

'Yes, Grayling. But be careful. This one has strongly *unusual* tendencies.'

'Does she?' Grayling's eyes narrowed. 'We can change that.'

Grayling was a tall, straight-backed man with a bristly moustache. His eyes were pebble-hard as they glared down at Grace.

'Do as Mr Grayling tells you,' Mrs Bland said, and strode away.

'Follow me,' said Grayling.

'Where to?' Grace asked, not moving.

'You'll find out. It's perfectly Ordinary.' He pushed her in the middle of her back, forcing her into a long door-lined corridor. They stopped halfway down.

'Wait,' he ordered. He thumped the door, then slid a key into the lock. A girl of about Grace's age was standing to attention when they entered. She was trying not to yawn.

'Your new roommate. Show her what to do.'

'She's got to sleep underneath,' said the girl.

'I don't care,' said Grayling. He propelled Grace towards the girl, 'No messing about.' Then he pulled the door closed. It gave a metallic clang.

'Mine's the top one,' said the girl.

Grace only understood when the other girl climbed a little ladder to the top bunk bed. She lay on her side, watching Grace who had not yet moved.

Grace made observations. There was a high window, which was far too small to escape from. Through it she could see the top of a wire fence. In the corner was a toilet cubicle, a sink, and a bar of colourless soap and two plastic cups. She crossed to the sink and gulped some water. The walls and floor were concrete, with a worn charcoal-coloured rug next to the bunk beds. A dim light bulb hung from the centre of the ceiling.

'Where are we?'

'A bedroom. Obviously,' said the girl.

Grace thought of her own cosy little bedroom, with her books, computer and microscope, and the cheerful yellow of her wall, before her mother had made her paint it.

'What's your name?' said Grace.

'Is asking questions all you do?' the girl said.

'I'm only asking your name.'

'Ann.'

'Ann,' Grace repeated, suddenly very tired.

'It is a good Ordinary name,' said Ann, 'and I am lucky to have it because it's Mrs Bland's name too. They gave it to me when I came here.'

'When was that?' asked Grace.

'Weeks ago,' said Ann.

'Do your parents know you are here?'

'D'uh! Mrs Bland knows I'm here. That's all that counts.'

'My name is Grace,' she said, after a pause.

'Whatever,' said Ann.

'What where you called before they called you Ann?' asked Grace.

'Not important.'

'You must know!'

For a moment, a troubled expression crossed Ann's face. 'I think... I think it was...' She was struggling.

Knuckles rapped angrily on the door.

'I said no messing about!' Grayling shouted.

The light went off. Two even dimmer lights lit up in the bunk beds.

'Just go to bed,' whispered Ann, turning her bed light out.

The sheets were clean but the blanket on the bed was thin and scratchy. Under her pillow was a booklet, and Grace held up to the feeble glow. 'Welcome to Charcoal House' was printed in small dark letters. On its cover was a picture of Mrs Bland, and inside there were flattering photos of her with smiling supporters. Alongside these pictures were printed some of Mrs Bland's sayings.

Grace read one at random.

Ordinary is as Ordinary does. It's no good just saying you are Ordinary, you have to be Ordinary too. That means if you see anything unusual in yourself or your family, you must come down on it hard. Only that way can you feel truly happy, and bring peace and prosperity to our country.

Grace threw it under the bed in disgust. *Somehow,* she thought, *I am going to escape.*

She turned her bed light off. Once Grace's eyes had adjusted, she could see a small square of moonlight on the grey floor.

'Goodnight,' she called up to the girl on the bunk above her.

Ann did not reply.

Chapter 5

A slip of the mask

'Where am I?'

Footsteps and shouting in the echoey corridor had woken Grace, but she did not want to open her eyes. Their door was unlocked and opened. A man shouted, 'Up! Get up! Ordinary is as Ordinary does!' and was gone.

Bleary eyed, Grace peeped up at the mattress sagging over her head. The memory of being dragged to this dismal bedroom last night returned.

'Get up,' said Ann.

'What happens now?' asked Grace.

'Breakfast, of course.'

Grace had slept in her clothes. She threw off the blanket and waited for Ann to finish dressing. The corridor sounded full of children. As soon as they stepped out, however, Ann met another girl who seemed to be her friend. They turned their backs on Grace.

I don't care, Grace told herself, *I'm going to escape*. She followed the crush of about sixty boys and girls hurrying towards the smell of cooking.

Her stomach rumbled. She had eaten little at the Grey Ball. The small canteen had a poster with Mrs Bland on it holding a green apple with a bite out of it. On the poster were these words: *Sensible food for sensible children, the foundation of an Ordinary life.*

Grace joined the queue that snaked beside three rows of beige tables, with battered wooden chairs. Just in front of her was a small boy who stood with his arms wrapped around himself. She was thinking of something to say to him, when the serving hatches opened to reveal big catering trays of baked beans and scrambled eggs and sausages. Everyone could see the food, but nobody moved.

'Silence!' roared Grayling, as he entered the room, his hard shoes tapping on the floor.

The children (who had hardly been noisy at all) hushed.

After Grayling, Nick, Rick and Dick swaggered in, moving to the front of the queue.

Everyone bent their heads, so Grace copied them.

'For what we are about to receive...' began Mr Grayling in a commanding voice.

'May we all give thanks to Mrs Ann Bland,' they chanted in response.

This was the signal. After Mrs Bland's sons were served, everyone else raced forward, and two women behind the hatch began spooning out food.

Grace was at the end of the queue. Other students arriving later had simply pushed in before her. By the time she had reached the serving hatch, nothing nice to eat remained.

'Dry toast and splosh for you,' said a woman in a grey apron, sliding two slices of toast and a mug of weak tea towards her.

'Can I have some butter?' asked Grace.

'No. No butter,' said the woman. 'No margarine or fancy spread neither.' Before Grace could ask anything else, the woman abruptly pulled down the shutter between them.

There was nowhere left to sit except for a space on the table Nick, Rick and Dick were using. Grace felt everyone's eyes on her as she sat down. Ann, who was nearby on a full table, whispered to her friend. The other girl sniggered.

The brothers did not look at her. They had enjoyed breakfast with fruit juice and yoghurt and eggs and sausages and rounds of toast and jam. Grace gazed enviously at their plates, until Nick, who was the biggest boy, glared at her. What was worse, the middle brother Rick had only toyed with his food, and had left lots.

Spoilt, thought Grace as she wolfed her dry toast. Before she had a chance to finish her tea, Mr Grayling marched back into the canteen.

'Plates away!' he ordered.

The effect was instantaneous: chair legs scraped as everyone, even if they had not finished, jumped up from their seats.

'Move it!' bellowed Grayling.

Everyone hurried off, except for Grace. She had no idea what to do next or where to go. The canteen staff would be no help, clattering noisily in the kitchen. Only Grayling was left, and he was reading a message on his phone.

'Excuse me,' she said.

'Wait!' Satisfied with whatever he was doing, he put his phone away. 'Grey Brown,' he said looming over her. 'Mrs Bland says you need special attention: unusual, she called you.'

He pushed his mouth close to Grace. 'I'll give you *Mrs Bland is a dangerous lunatic who should be strapped to a giant boulder and catapulted to the moon!*' His moustache was like thin wires against her ear.

'We will break you,' he straightened up again. His tone was factual. 'You will learn obedience, like the other children who this morning will study the Ordinary thoughts of Mrs Bland. Later there will be the Mrs Bland quiz, which will pose questions about her opinions. And this afternoon,' he continued, 'there is an art class, and the opportunity to paint a portrait of our leader. The most Ordinary one will be given this prize.'

Grayling drew a book from under his arm called *Essentials of Ordinary life*, by Mrs Bland. On its cover was a picture of his leader pointing her finger with a stern face.

'It looks stupid,' said Grace.

Grayling's face went purple.

'We'll soon see who is being stupid.' Mr Grayling grabbed her arm, and marched her along the corridor. She was doing her best to keep up, but from time to time he would give an extra hard pull, and her toes would scuff along the floor until she could find her feet.

They stopped outside a black door, with the word *ISOLATION* stencilled on it in light grey letters. Grayling, still gripping Grace, unlocked the door and thrust her into a cell with one beige table and a four charcoal grey chairs. There was a thin blanket in one corner, and a bucket in the other. At her back, a key turned and a bolt was drawn to lock her in. High on the door was a spyhole through which an adult could watch anyone in the room.

Grace was panting, sprawled on the floor from where she had been thrown. One of her knees was grazed, but it only bled a little. 'I've got to escape,' she muttered to herself. But there were no windows to climb through, nor anywhere to hide.

'Escape, did you say?' A cold voice rang outside the door, which was laboriously unlocked again and swung open.

It was Mrs Bland.

'You will never escape.'

Grace flinched back against the wall. Nothing happened, so she opened her eyes. Only then did Mrs Bland slap her hard in the face, and push her into a plastic chair. Mr Grayling returned, smiling unpleasantly.

'Apparently you're stupid,' he said.

'Stupid, am I?' said Mrs Bland, not taking her eyes off the girl.

Grace said nothing.

'I'll give you one thing, you're a challenge. But I will win, of course, and rapidly. I have far too many things of international importance to achieve today, to be wasting time with a barbaric girl.' Mrs Bland sat down opposite Grace, and stared at her across the table.

A cloak, so dark that it was almost black hung from her shoulders. On her lapel was pinned a sparkling brooch. Her fingers too, were resplendent with diamonds.

Diamonds are one of the hardest natural substances, thought Grace.

'Mr Grayling, thank you. I will deal personally with her education for a few minutes,' Mrs Bland said. Before the door was closed, she had grabbed both of Grace's pigtails in one fist, pulling Grace's head backwards so she could stare into her face.

Up close, Mrs Bland was beautiful, and scented with perfume. Even her breath was minty. Her eyes betrayed her, however; they were full of reckless hate. Grace gulped with terror.

'Fascinating,' said Mrs Bland, releasing Grace's pigtails. 'Let there be no secrets between us, Grace, for secrets are designed to be kept. And, unfortunately...' she smirked, 'unfortunately you won't have enough time to keep anything. Tell me, Grace, what did you want to become? Did you have plans for this Ordinary little life of yours?'

'Yes,' said Grace, 'I want to be a biologist.'

'A biologist? How *unusual*,' Mrs Bland said. '*Don't* turn away, girl,' she ordered icily. 'So I'm to deprive the world of a *scientist*,' she said, as if the word tasted bitter. She appeared to be thinking hard. 'But you might have one use. You are a fine example of all that's wrong with Ordinary people. Although I have half a mind to simply delete you from the school records and be done with it.'

'Delete me?' said Grace, nervously.

Mrs Bland was thinking, and eventually said aloud, 'Yes, yes. My boys need to be reminded of the more difficult decisions they will have to take.' She released Grace like a dropped cloth. 'Grace,' she laughed, 'I'll use you in an experiment. A perfect end to the career of a *biologist*.'

The door slammed, and was locked again. Breathing hard, Grace heard Mrs Bland shouting for Grayling outside. 'Bring me my boys, Mr Grayling.'

Minutes later, Mrs Bland returned with Nick, her eldest son, and Dick, the youngest. Both glanced at Grace with little curiosity.

'Where's Rick?' asked their mother.

'Nowhere to be found,' said Grayling, stepping in after.

'Hmm,' said Mrs Bland, scowling. She turned to her other sons. 'I have a special lesson today. I know this might be a bit upsetting, but I am going to expose you to this... this *girl*,' she said, pointing at Grace.

'Why, Mother?' asked Nick.

'She is an example of everything we should not be: wilful, unusual and twisted. I even suspect her of *originality*,' said Mrs Bland, 'and what is originality, Nick?'

'Forbidden, Mother,' said Nick, 'because Ordinary people should never try to be original.'

'Quite right! Originality must be eliminated. It never brings anyone happiness. You can see what it has done for this female,' she said. She stood between her sons, stroking their hair and beaming down at their dull faces.

It made Grace feel sick.

'Where is Rick, my darlings?' asked Mrs Bland again. 'He has orders to stay with you at all times.'

'I don't know, Mother,' said Dick, 'I'm sorry.'

Mrs Bland put her hand on the boys' shoulders. 'Never mind. After all, it will fall to you two, not Rick, to deal with people like this wretch. Today I want both of you to see the depths Ordinary people can plumb if they ignore my leadership. I want you to come to a decision about her. But, my darlings, be careful. She is dangerous.'

She strode out, leaving the two boys standing over Grace.

'Well,' said Nick, 'explain yourself.'

'I don't have to say anything to you,' said Grace.

'Mother!' called out Dick.

Mrs Bland, who was still just outside talking to Grayling, stepped in.

'She won't do as we say,' said Dick.

'Stubborn girl,' said his mother. 'Her future is in your hands.' The door shut again.

All the frightening things Grace had thought bubbled up inside her. But instead of screaming with terror, she laughed.

'Make me,' she said. The more angry the boys' ridiculous faces became, the harder she laughed.

'Stop it or you'll be sorry!' shouted Nick. But Grace would not, or could not, stop.

'I have nothing to say,' she replied. 'I have done nothing wrong. I have been taken by your horrible mother to this disgusting place and I want to go home.'

'What did you call our mother?' asked Dick, shocked.

'I said she was horrible, and she is.'

Grace could hear Mrs Bland's heels in the concrete corridor. As she approached, it sounded like she was dragging something. The door was wrenched open, and she was back in the cell with them, hauling Rick by the collar of his jacket. He seemed scared.

'So boys, what have you decided?'

Dick nudged his older brother with a smirk.

'We think,' said Nick, smiling nastily at Grace, 'that you should delete her.'

'Good boys,' said Mrs Bland. 'I am considering it. But two out of three is not the same as three out of three is it? We must all come to the same opinion, we don't want to be original, now do we?'

'No, Mother,' mumbled the boys.

She shook Rick. 'Now tell me what you were doing. If it's that tree again...' She flew into a sudden icy fury, 'I will NOT have you climbing that tree. Do NOT disobey me again!'

Rick's mouth was open but he said nothing. Staring into his face, with his braces gleaming at her, Mrs Bland came to a decision.

'The rest of us are going to leave Rick to talk to this girl himself, and come to his own conclusion. For he can be a useful little sneak.'

Nick and Dick followed their mother out, and as their footsteps receded in the corridor, Grace knew that Rick did not frighten her. Although they were now locked in together, she imagined a wall between them, and that she was safe behind it.

She observed the boy. If she had had her tiny turquoise notebook with her, she might have written down how uncomfortable he appeared, and how he fidgeting with his braces. *Was he was in more trouble than she was?* she wondered.

'Which one are you again?' asked Grace.

'Rick,' he said. Something had made him answer her.

'Do you like climbing trees?' asked Grace. The scientist in her was curious, because the more she examined Rick, the less like the others he seemed.

'So what if I do?' he said, fiddling once more with his tooth brace.

'It's just a bit...' Then, and she didn't quite know why, she said: 'If you ask me, climbing trees is a bit *unusual.*'

Rick gave a violent start of surprise.

The tooth brace jerked loose.

Grace saw that not only the brace, but the teeth seemed to have come loose too. Fumbling, Rick panicked. Suddenly, the spitty plastic and metal fell onto the table. His mouth opened wide in dismay.

Teeth!

Rick had a mouthful of needle-thin teeth, that had been cleverly disguised by his braces. Grace now saw that his face was very *unusual.* In fact it seemed a bit similar to a bat's face...

Normal!

This was incredible. Rick, the son of Mrs Bland the self-styled leader of Ordinary people, was Normal.

Rick scrabbled madly, and shoved the disguise back into his mouth.

But it was too late. Grace knew his secret.

Without warning, Mrs Bland stormed in. She must have been watching through the spyhole. Startled, Rick dropped his false teeth yet again.

His mother gasped. 'Fool!' She lashed at her son, knocking him to the floor. 'You disgusting fool!'

'Leave him alone!' shouted Grace.

Mrs Bland froze. 'You!' she gasped in fury, sinking her manicured talons into Grace's arm.

On his hands and knees on the floor Rick found his brace. He pushed it back into his mouth.

'Grayling! Grayling!' Mrs Bland shouted. Grace writhed in her grasp as the man rushed to his leader's side.

'This... this... little jinx!'

'Understood, ma'am,' said Grayling. 'Should I...'

'Oh yes. Let's delete her! Make the preparations.'

Grayling left immediately.

'And as for you!' Mrs Bland said to Rick with fury. 'Get out of my sight. I will deal with you later.'

Rick scurried off, his hand cupped over his mouth.

Alone with Grace, Mrs Bland loomed menacingly over her. She saw how this girl was opposing her with all her will. Grace had bunched her fists and, just for a second, Mrs Bland wavered, as if Grace had sparked something like admiration in her cold heart.

'Seeing as you adore Normals so much,' she said, her face hardening, 'I'll leave you in the dark. They all love the dark.'

She was locked in again. This time, however, Mrs Bland had extinguished the light in the windowless room.

Grace sank down to the floor in the corner of the cell, waiting to be deleted.

Chapter 6

Deleted

A giant cursor erasing the letters G-R-A-C-E one by one? After spending about half an hour in the dark *ISOLATION* cell wondering what being *deleted* actually meant, Grace's mind started playing tricks. Ghostly fingers poked at her arms and shoulders through the walls of the corner she was wedged into. Then she began to worry there was not enough oxygen in the cell to breathe. Later, she thought she heard a rat creeping towards her.

'Grace Brown, just stop it!' Hearing her own voice helped.

She tried an experiment. She closed her eyes, and imagined that she was in a cinema watching a movie. On the screen was an autumn wood. She stepped into the image, crunched the glorious gold, red and orange leaves underfoot. The darkness of the room seemed nothing compared to all the beautiful light inside her.

Dazzled.

The sudden harsh light made Grace blink. Mrs Bland entered, accompanied by two men. Their heads and faces were hidden inside woollen balaclavas, but their eyes peered eagerly out of holes in the fabric, and there were slits for their mouths and noses too.

'Enjoy the dark?' Mrs Bland said.

'I did,' said Grace.

'No surprise. Such behaviour is why you were in trouble in the first place. Are you sure you're not some Normal little witch?'

'Are you sure *you're* not?' Grace flashed back at her. She saw a moment's doubt in the wicked woman's eyes. Mrs Bland raised her hand to slap her again. Defiantly, Grace did not flinch away but glared up her.

Mrs Bland caught herself. Grace thought she saw something in her face soften for a second. But then it snuffed out. She barked an order to the men. 'Bring her to the courtyard, and be quick about it.'

One of the faceless men grabbed at Grace. A nightmarish scramble followed. For a few moments, Grace was too fast. She dodged between the table legs, evading their grasping hands until one of the men simply lifted the table up, and the other grabbed her wrists. She kicked out at a man's shins, making him swear nastily inside his hood. The next second she was trapped. The two men hoisted her into the air, and clamped Grace's arms and legs with their strong hands.

They banged out of the cell opposite an oil painting of Mrs Bland, and rushed Grace along the corridor. At some double doors one of the men booted them open, and they carried Grace outside.

The air felt cold. Grace shivered, as they entered the soulless courtyard. Dozens of subdued people had gathered in the far corner near the single tree. Around them, on all four sides, were the blank walls of Charcoal House.

Grace saw Mrs Bland emerge from the throng and, next to her, Mr Grayling with his straight back. All three brothers were there too. As she was carried towards them, she spotted that Mr Grayling was openly carrying a handgun. There were many other people, adults and children. Some were wearing grey hoods, others had balaclavas like the men who were hauling her forwards.

'She's here, Mother!' The high voice of Mrs Bland's youngest son floated towards them. A bell began to toll. Grace was marched across to face Mrs Bland again.

'Why isn't she tied?' Mrs Bland's voice rang out harshly.

'Apologies, ma'am, we were told to hurry.'

'Well do it now, and be quick!' she said impatiently.

Grace's arms were twisted behind her back. Her hands were bound by a band of tough plastic that bit into her wrists.

The crowd parted to let them through. Some of the children were there too, with their faces uncovered. One was Ann, whose room Grace had shared. Her expression was bored despite the hushed excitement all around her.

Mrs Bland called out, 'Not so full of your unusual *rudeness* now, are you?'

Grace was led to an enormous bird's nest of branches and planks. There was going to be a bonfire.

Slowly, she somehow understood that this fire would be for her. She looked at the sky above the roof of Charcoal House. It was flushed with the colours of the setting sun. It seemed painfully beautiful. Was it the last thing she would see?

They can't stop the colours, she thought.

The people formed a semicircle behind their leader.

'Bring her to me,' said Mrs Bland.

The bell stopped tolling, and Grace was dragged forwards, and pushed onto her knees. Her skin hurting on the gritty concrete.

'Grace Brown. You will never become Grey Brown, will you?' Mrs Bland sounded almost admiring for a moment. 'Grace Brown, we have found that you are a danger to our country and to Ordinary people everywhere. You must be deleted.'

Some of the hooded members in the crowd began to chant. *Delete the witch! Delete the witch!*

'You are a witch,' said Mrs Bland tonelessly.

Escape! Grace's mind screamed the word at her. Frantically, she tried to wriggle free of the men. If only she could get to her feet and run!

One of the men chuckled. All they had to do was lean on her shoulders to keep her down on her knees.

'Witch!' came shouted voices. 'Delete her!'

'And how do we delete witches?' asked Mrs Bland.

'By fire!' the voices answered.

'And who am I?' Mrs Bland called out to her followers.

'The Hammer of Witches!'

'The Hammer of Witches!' she thundered back at them. '*Malleus Maleficarium.*'

At this, another man in a balaclava stepped out of the crowd. He was carrying a long wooden stake. Grace was roughly pulled to her feet. Her arms, still tied behind her back, were hooped around the stake, which was then twisted and set into the ground. Sliding her arms up the pole, they lifted her onto an old wooden stool so everyone could clearly see her.

'Now set the fire,' Grayling ordered.

I'm going to die, Grace thought. The stool wobbled under her feet, and her wrists, now behind the pole, were painful and her hands were going numb. Frantically, her eyes flitted from Grayling with his gun, to the hooded men now lighting the fire. And there was Mrs Bland. She was grinning, with an insane green gleam in her eyes. Her three sons were beside her. and they were flanked by as many as eighty people.

'Begin the inferno!' shrieked Mrs Bland, her eyes flashing with excitement.

The mob gave a full-throated roar of approval as the first flames began to lick the wood.

I'm going to die, Grace thought again, as fire leapt from twig to branch to plank, and sprang up in hot tongues of yellow and orange.

A shock! Every hair on her head and arms stood on end. Although she was petrified by the fire, it was not fear that had done this. It was a weird sound in the wind, like the blast bursting from the throats of brazen trumpets and then a rumbling, not of thunder, but a kind of music. The disturbance in the air had come from far away and was not an Ordinary at all. It was a mystifying signal, an invisible wave that rolled magically across the country. It was a warning. It was a hope.

Mrs Bland screamed. She clamped her hands to her ears and fell heavily to her knees. Her shoulders jerking in spasms.

Confusion gripped the square. Hearing nothing themselves, the masked and hooded adults were bewildered, and the students of Charcoal House fell silent. What was wrong with their leader? Two of the three boys, Nick and Dick, bent over their mother with anxious faces.

Do something! With fierce new strength, Grace struggled against the plastic cuffs but they only sliced more painfully into her wrists. Her brain was sprinting. She saw Rick was sprawled on the floor like his mother.

Two of the older students ran to help Rick, but when they neared him they recoiled in fear. Something very out of the Ordinary was happening.

The shape of Rick's face had subtly changed, seeming oddly snouty. His brace had been spat from his mouth, and he was holding it numbly. *R-r-rip!* His clothes were tearing; his grey blazer split in half and fell from him. Something was tearing through his shirt.

Vast wings began to unfurl from his sides. Mrs Bland screamed again, pointing at her son.

'Delete him!' she shouted to Grayling. 'Shoot the impostor!'

Without hesitation, Grayling levelled his gun, and took aim at Rick. He had never disobeyed Mrs Bland before. Unless… Did Mrs Bland really mean him to shoot her son? Had she not just been taken ill?

He wavered for a second, ambushed by doubt, just as Rick scrambled into the air.

'Must I shoot him myself?' Mrs Bland sprang to her feet, snatching Grayling's handgun to aim at her own son who was already turning sharply above the single tree.

A shot, two shots, cracked out. Rick evaded them with rapid flaps of his wings and an incredible burst of speed. Blasts of erratic gunfire followed, but his swooping, curling evasions saved him.

Mrs Bland was incandescent with rage.

'This is her witchcraft!' she said, pointing at Grace, who was cowering in terror from the roaring flames. A wall of shrivelling heat had sprung up around the girl.

Too hot!

Grace screamed. Mrs Bland laughed crazily.

But something had seized Grace Brown. She was being hauled vertically so that the loop of her arms slid up the stake.

Airborne!

With giddying speed, she was whooshed upwards, and away from the flames. Up, up, up, into the smoky, bullet-filled sky.

Chapter 7

A mother's son

Grace's face was pressed into damp leaves. Something was snuffling at her wrists.

Rick moved away, having freed the girl's hands with his sharp teeth. He spat out a thick shred of plastic.

'Awake now?' he asked. His voice sounded firmer without the false teeth and braces in his mouth.

'What happened?' asked Grace. She sat up, rubbing her sore wrists and flicking a clump of mud from her face.

'I rescued you.'

'But I thought you hated me,' she said.

Rick shrugged his bulky shoulders, visible through the rags of his shirt.

'Were they really were going to burn me?' Grace asked.

'Yes. My beloved mother branded you a witch. She wants you dead. Now she wants me dead too.'

'But you're her son. She wouldn't kill you, would she?'

Rick's black eyes glittered. 'She just tried to shoot me,' he said. 'Mothers. What are they worth? Your one just handed you over to mine; no second thoughts. If you take my advice, don't trust anyone except yourself.'

Grace scrambled to her feet, and brushed herself down. Thinking about her mother, and her father, was too complicated. She missed them. She also hated them.

It was nearly dark. They were standing on a high hill and the lights of Charcoal House were far below them in the valley. They watched as two cars sped away, their headlights bright in the twilight until they were hidden by trees. Metal gates in the barbed wire perimeter had opened, and six men with flashlights and Alsatian dogs ran out. Some melted into the woods, and others made their way behind the building into open fields. The sound of barking carried in the stillness.

Rick laughed scornfully.

'Catch me with those?' he said. 'I could fly to France if I wanted.' Defiant, he kicked at something on the ground. Not a stone, but his gleaming false teeth. Even in the chaos, habit had made him snatch them up from the courtyard.

'What happened to you?'

'Nothing happened to me,' said Rick.

'You *are* Normal,' said Grace. 'Doesn't your mother hate Normal people?'

'Oh she despises them. She hates me, because I've always been like this. I have to pretend all the time. You see I'm different to the perfect boys. Nick and Dick. The perfectly Ordinary boys, the perfectly stupid boys.'

He stooped down and picked up his false teeth from where he'd kicked them.

'Never again!' he shouted, and he threw them as far as he could into a bank of stinging nettles further down the hill.

'Are you're going to be yourself now?' asked Grace.

Rick said nothing, but his eyes were red.

Barking drifted up from the valley. Perhaps by coincidence, the dogs were now racing in their direction.

'Please take me with you.'

'Why? You're not Normal. I want to follow that sound I heard...' he said. 'I can't really explain why, but I need to find out what it means.'

Harsh perimeter lights of Charcoal House had begun to stare out across the shadow of the valley.

'Well I can't go back to that place.' Grace shuddered. 'And I heard it too, didn't I?' She also remembered the weird and wonderful sound that had brought Mrs Bland to her knees.

Rick sighed. 'Okay. I won't leave a child to the dogs,' he said, extending his wings again, as if judging the air.

'A child?' said Grace, stung. 'I bet I'm the same age as you.'

Rick laughed at her strangely.

'I'm a lot older than I look,' he said.

'But you're a boy, aren't you?'

'Yes. I will always be a boy,' he sighed.

Grace did not quite understand. But Rick was talking again.

'I will take you. But you'll have to climb onto my back. My arms aren't as strong as my wings.'

Grace stood behind Rick and looped her arms, which were already painful from being tied, loosely around his neck. His wings gave an enormous beat and she closed her eyes and clung on as tight as she could.

The cool dark air streamed around them. Finally Grace found the courage to open her eyes again as they swooped, just above the treetops and cosy roofs of a little village.

Rick's back was hot with effort. He was exceptionally agile in the air, dodging around trees and under wires at the last moment. Sometimes, almost dislodging Grace, he snatched moths and other large insects from the air with his mouth.

For what seemed like hours, the dark countryside scrolled below them. Rick avoided towns and larger villages. Now, however, they skimmed across the vast lawns of an old country house. They dipped past its windows, and Grace could glimpse people gathered in the rooms.

They veered away, across an ornamental pond.

'Please stop!' said Grace. 'My arms are killing me.' They had been hurting very much, but her need to be as far away as possible from Mrs Bland was stronger than pain.

Rick wheeled downwards, and they landed heavily next to a bench. Though the gardens were well tended, a patch nearby had been left as a natural meadow.

'Blackberries!' said Grace. Although many were wizened, a handful or two of deliciously ripe berries were still to be had. She ate them hungrily, after blowing off the spiders. The scratches the brambles had given her were worth it. It reminded her of her father, before *The Big Parent Change* of course, raiding country hedges to fill plastic bags with ripe fruit to make into jam.

Rick laughed at her purple hands and lips.

'How much further?' asked Grace.

'The sound is stronger now, so we are nearer,' said Rick, but Grace could hear nothing now.

'An hour, maybe?' said Rick. 'I'd be a lot quicker if I didn't have you,' he added, rubbing his shoulders. 'I can fly for another hour, if you can hold on that long.'

'Of course,' said Grace, although her arms ached, and she was shivering with cold. Soon they were flying above the great orange glow of London. Sometimes Grace could hear traffic and, once, music drifted up from the streets. They flew over rooftops, tall office buildings, bright high streets and shopping malls, and motorways flowing with red and white light. All the time, Rick climbed higher in the sky, and he began to follow the slow curls of the River Thames. It was a beautiful sight.

Horribly, and without warning, Grace lost her grip.

She fell, wingless and alone. The dark water of the river raced up to meet her.

Rick thudded painfully into her side, his wings barely extended.

'Hold on!' he shouted, straining to parachute their fall.

Gasping in pain and shock, Grace clung to his neck as he levelled off in the air. The park below seemed familiar. Trying to calm herself she observed it was her part of London, with the High Street and supermarkets. Her home! And the lights are on! But in a flash the vision was behind her.

I can escape. I can go home to Mum and Dad now, Grace thought. But a cold voice answered for her. *Yes, and they will send you straight back to Mrs Bland.*

'The sound! It's coming from here!' Rick shouted, pointing towards a building festooned with towers, and turrets that branched into the sky. Despite its being so close to where she lived, Grace had never seen a building like this before. It was ringed by bonfires.

They were close now. They plunged into hot, smoky air, and heard angry shouting from below. Rick coughed violently in the smoke. Grace gripped as hard as her exhausted arms could manage.

'There!' she cried, daring to loosen her grip and point to a platform on one of the turrets.

Rick swooped, but their landing was clumsy. They sprawled apart on the floor.

Grace could barely feel her arms. In pain, and panting for breath, she lay on her back looking up at the sky. Rick was still coughing, but his wings were already furled away. He slumped with the exhaustion he had not let himself feel till now.

Eventually, he let out a high-pitched, chittering laugh of relief.

A trapdoor in the platform opened with a creak, just two metres away from Grace. From it emerged two elegant gentlemen. They sported purple suits, and flamboyant waistcoats. One of them had a monocle in his eye socket.

'Well, Bonaparte,' said one, 'a nice view all of a sudden from my Tower. A Tower, may I remind you, whose existence you have always questioned, and I...'

The gentleman's silver-rimmed monocle popped from his eye socket.

'Now then, what do we have here?'

'Skelton, old stick, it is not *what* do we have here, it is *whom* do we have here?' said Bonaparte, the other gentleman.

They studied the children.

'Surely that's not Sunny?' said Skelton.

'Of course it isn't, you numbskull. Sunny would be well over 100 years old now.'

'You're correct,' Skelton said irritably. He peered keenly at Grace. 'Well, well! Bonaparte, we *do* know this girl. It is Grace Brown!'

'Yes,' said Bonaparte sourly, 'the one with the toothy sister. And here is a boy of some sort who, unless I am very much mistaken, appears perfectly Normal.'

Skelton replaced his monocle and glinted it in Rick's direction. 'Young man, are you all right?'

'Yes, sir,' said Rick.

'Did you hear that, Bonaparte? Manners are so rare these days – as you can tell from all this *rudeness* going on below. Young man, I have two questions for you. The first: did your sharp bat-boy ears hear the summons from my Tower? And secondly I want to know who your parents are? I might know them.'

'I heard the call,' said Rick. 'Came from here, did it? I just had to follow it. And as for my parents... Well...'

'Spit it out, you whipperflapper,' said Bonaparte.

'His mother is Mrs Bland,' said Grace.

'She's your *mother*?' said Bonaparte.

Instantly, he seized the exhausted boy and dragged him towards the crenellated edge of the platform.

'Bonaparte!' Skelton said. 'What on earth are you doing?'

'Chucking him over the edge of course.'

'But he was summoned here by the Tower itself, the boy's clearly Normal,' Skelton growled. 'Plus, you walnut-brain, the boy can fly.'

'True.' Bonaparte smiled nastily, showing all his teeth. 'So I'll brain him.' He grabbed Rick by his hair, and dragged him over to a corner of the ramparts. Seizing the boy's whimpering head, he took aim.

'Stop it!' Grace shouted.

'Stop it? She must have been brainwashed too,' said Bonaparte wildly. 'Grab her, Skelton!'

Chapter 8

Three little words

During the short time Grace spent in Charcoal House, life for many people was going on *as usual*. That does not mean nothing was happening. For what is *usual* for some would be extremely hard for others to imagine, let alone live through.

But before you read about what was happening to Skelton and Bonaparte, you should know a few more things about Rick, the boy who is about to get his brains dashed out.

For many years Rick was Mrs Bland's only son. Yes that's right. Her *only* son.

On the rare occasions Rick was seen in the company of the famous politician, she would barely acknowledge him, and would certainly not touch him.

'Ah yes,' Mrs Bland would say. 'That's Richard, Rick we call him. He's my nephew – well I *call* him my nephew – he's really the orphaned son of a loyal family servant.'

Everyone believed her. Smarmy guests believed her, important political figures believed her; they thought it was just like Mrs Bland to take care of Ordinary people less fortunate than herself. After allowing themselves an indulgent smile at the boy, some tutting sympathetically over his unusually heavy tooth braces, they would turn away again to discuss economics or immigration or the Normal problem.

On the few occasions he tried to speak, his mother would give him a stare that turned his tongue to stone, and he would slink away unnoticed.

Rick did not complain. For he spent his early childhood locked away from sight, being whispered about and scolded by servants. It was only when he was old enough to wear his excruciating braces and false teeth, that he was ever glimpsed in public. For it was vital that Rick should appear Ordinary, despite the constant torment of having his jaw forced down, and his mouth filled with metal, plastic and false teeth.

As Rick grew older, it soon became clear he would grow no taller than a eleven-year-old. Nor did his face change. His wings, however, continued to strengthen despite the special measures taken to strap them to his back.

Once before, Mrs Bland had tried to seize power. She had failed. She was too ambitious, she struck too quickly and was defeated. Retreating to her mansion in the countryside, she had licked her wounds and invented new lies. Her humiliation tormented her, and she used all her weapons of charm, deceit and manipulation to plot her revenge.

It was around this time she realised that her embarrassingly Normal child could, in fact, become a useful tool in her campaign. She trained Rick to become her secret sneak thief.

He would be ordered to fly to the houses of her rivals, especially Normal rivals. Clinging all night to rooftops, or the glass and steel of office block walls, Rick would place microphones to record the conversations going on within.

He did not understand half of what he was sent to hear. He reported back as best he could, and his recordings were priceless. Sometimes, to please his mother, he broke in to steal important papers, mobile phones, computers or just money. He was an excellent thief, able to fling himself from windows or rooftops to make his escape.

As he grew older, his mother contrived a new skill. She called it *remote control*.

Against his will, Rick found himself being steered through corridors into private places. He watched his hands sift through secret papers, and hack into confidential computers to steal information.

He fought back sometimes. Occasionally he could block her intruding mind, and tear himself away from the path she forced him down. This only led to trouble later. Defying his mother was dangerous. He had the scars to prove it.

Despite this, he learned to tolerate her remote control. For the first time in his life she seemed to value him. He had become her eyes and ears in the night. He was useful. He was wanted.

But one April morning, Rick learnt about love.

For the first time in his life, he was summoned to his mother's bedside.

In the past, if she had wanted to speak to him, she came to his mean little bedroom away from the main parts of the house. She would sit on the corner of his bed with distaste, and list his instructions.

Wary, Rick approached Mrs Bland's personal assistant, a round bustling lady her mistress called *Dumpling*. She was arranging bunches of flowers in the corridor outside Mrs Bland's private rooms.

'You can go in now,' said Dumpling.

Rick paused in the doorway of a luxurious room. He had never seen it before. His feet sank into a white carpet, and his fingers trailed over the plush chairs and heavy velvet curtains. He caught a glimpse of an enormous walk-in wardrobe lined with glamorous clothes. It was like somewhere a film star or a princess would sleep.

'It's beautiful,' his voice was an awed whisper.

'Yes, isn't he?' said Mrs Bland.

At first Rick didn't understand.

Isn't he?

Her face had an odd expression that Rick had never seen before, softer, and more beautiful today than he had ever seen it.

At that moment Rick realised that the 'he' his mother was talking about was the thing she held in her arms. A tiny baby wrapped in a snow-white blanket.

'You should meet him. This is my son: he is called Nick.' She pulled the baby close to her face, and kissed its wrinkly forehead. It gurgled with satisfaction.

'Nick is my son,' she repeated. 'He is perfect. Perfectly, perfectly Ordinary. Rick, you now have new duties. Make sure no harm comes to this beautiful boy of mine.'

'But... Aren't I your son too?' Rick blurted out.

A grimace of distaste marred his mother's features.

'I have my *perfect* son, now,' said Mrs Bland. 'A boy to be proud of. His name is Nick, and I love him.'

I love him.

Three little words that scarred Rick forever.

Part II

The Second Kind of Darkness

Chapter 9

The siege begins

On the morning of 31 October, as Grace Brown was waking up in Charcoal House and hurrying hungrily towards the canteen, Skelton and Bonaparte were repainting Skelton's garden fence. They used the perfectly Normal colours of purple and orange to cover the graffiti that had been sprayed overnight. As well as obscenities and *Normals Out* slogans, today's graffiti included a picture of a cat with six legs. It was a cartoon of Fibula, Skelton's housemate. She was outlined in black, with crosses for eyes and a dagger sunk in her head.

'In the head too!' Skelton said sadly, 'Not a place a *civilised* person would stab anyone.'

Bonaparte had an urge to laugh at how Fibula's lolling tongue had been scrawled. This soon wore off, however, when he saw the three men in grey across the road. Their hostile stares were unnerving.

Skelton and Bonaparte hurried indoors, past clumps of attractive thorns and a large pot of carnivorous plants which snapped lovingly at them as they approached. Skelton fondly stroked his fearsome, bat-faced door knocker, as he slid his skeleton key into the lock. The door gave a pleasingly Normal creak as they stepped in, followed by a doomy slam. The noise reverberated through the house.

Once inside, Skelton turned his key in his several extra locks, slid three big bolts, before he attached some chains. They were safe then to enjoy standing for a moment in the spot in the hallway that was always unnaturally cold.

Skelton's ancestral home was his pride and joy.

'A quick tour?' he would ask his visitors. Before they could say *no thanks*, they would be whisked around the house.

Naturally the tour would start in the kitchen. Walking straight ahead from the front door, ignoring a flight of stairs leading up on your left, and the door to the sitting room on your right, you would be lead into what Skelton called the heart of the house. It was a lovely dark kitchen lit by candles and gouts of fire from the hobs, and haunted by the smells of adventurous Normal cooking. Near the vast stove was a honeycomb of cobwebby cupboards. Some were full of heavy pots and pans, large plates and cutlery, others with sacks of dried provisions and a few tins. One or two were left totally empty apart from the corpses of dead bluebottles, and dust so thick that you could sign your name in it with a huge flourish. The fridge and deep freeze, however, were always loaded with food.

At the end of the kitchen was a back door leading to a modest city garden. This was also heavily bolted and chained, and if you were taking one of Skelton's tours you would notice that every window on the ground floor was barred with steel to prevent people breaking in.

Part of the huge kitchen was given over to everyday eating. Surrounded by a dozen chairs, the vast kitchen table was made of ancient oak, but scarred in two places by deep saw cuts. One of Skelton's ancestors had been a surgeon, and had left the table in a poor condition, with unpleasant stains that had resisted scrubbing for more than three hundred years.

The library of recipe books had been left to Skelton by his father, who had been a famous chef in Normal circles. According to Skelton, the fact that his father was always generously handing him a piece of mouse pie, or a plate of flash-fried tarantulas is why he was a lover of fine food to this day.

Bonaparte was equally a connoisseur of cuisine. Skelton maintained Bonaparte's obsession with eatables, however, was purely due to greed.

Near the back door, by the kitchen window, pots of straggly nettles and unusual fungi were cultivated. There were also decoratively dangling chains and flaps of leather to make things cosy.

Step out of the kitchen, and you will find yourself in the hallway, with a staircase leading up. Under the stairs is reputedly the most spacious cupboard of all, but it was never used. It had a circular door, dated 1603, which had been kept securely bolted and chained by Skelton, and his father before him, for over a hundred years.

At certain times of year, a few entirely Normal (but disconcerting) hisses could be heard coming from it, and a gnawing like teeth on wood.

'Rats?' Fibula, Skelton's six-legged feline housemate, would say hopefully, licking her lips.

'As big as warthogs by the sound of them,' Skelton would reply. But neither of them ever felt inclined to open the door to find out. The hissing sounded unpleasant and not at all like either rats or warthogs.

Opposite the cupboard under the stairs, was a living room containing three bulging, gold-coloured sofas, a ruby-red rug and a television. The walls were painted lizard green, and it was a good place to flop when Skelton had eaten too much to crawl upstairs to bed.

And as for upstairs… Our story will take you up there soon enough, but upstairs Skelton would have shown you a bathroom, three sleeping chambers and a Long Room, used for dining and entertaining. For Skelton, a home without guests was like a pie without filling. His most frequent guest and best friend was Bonaparte, who often staying for weeks at a time.

Skelton was not the only inhabitant. There was Fibula of course, and Fibula's distant cousin Tibia, who had only just moved in. Skelton was already having second thoughts about Tibia. The enormous tomcat was grumpy. He had battered ears, and stretched out around the house like one of those stuffed snakes Ordinary people put at the bottom of doors to block drafts.

Worse, Tibia was a cat of few words, and one thing Skelton liked was words. Soon enough, however, he would hear all too much from the newcomer.

Skelton and Bonaparte were standing in the kitchen, each finishing their third piece of pie. Every mouthful had brought a pleasurable crunch of small bones, for extra calcium. As they poked the last crumbs of pastry into their mouths heavy footsteps scuffed towards the front door. Something was thrust through the letterbox.

Moments later Fibula sprang into the kitchen with a flyer in her mouth.

'Mrrrrow mmmrible,' she said.

'Pardon?' said Skelton.

'Terrible,' Fibula said, having unclamped her teeth. 'Read this!'

URGENT ATTENTION!
OFFICIAL NOTICE FOR NORMAL HOUSEHOLDS

HALLOWEEN IS CANCELLED WITH IMMEDIATE EFFECT

- Anybody hosting or attending a 'Halloween' party WILL BE ARRESTED.
- Anybody seen trick-or-treating WILL BE ARRESTED.
- Anybody wearing colourful clothes WILL BE ARRESTED.
- Anybody behaving in a manner likely to cause disorder in public through inappropriate laughter, prank-playing, consuming chocolate, candies and sweets, or otherwise having 'fun' WILL BE ARRESTED.
- Normal people seen on the street WILL BE ARRESTED to prevent confusion.
- Anybody talking to a normal person on the street WILL BE ARRESTED.
- Pumpkins are prohibited. BY LAW.

HALLOWEEN IS BANNED.
BY ORDER OF MRS BLAND SIGNED 31st OCTOBER.

As Skelton read it aloud, Bonaparte began to tremble. 'They can't ban *Halloween*,' he said. 'It's tonight. They just can't *ban* it.'

'It's that Mrs Bland again,' said Skelton. 'She's the worst person in... OUCH!' A sudden, skewering pain in his thumbs had stopped him mid-flow. Bonaparte held up his thumbs in pained surprise, and a startled Fibula licked at her front paws.

'By the pricking of my thumbs...' Skelton said.

'...something wicked this way comes,' wailed Fibula.

Unless you are Normal person, or have Normal friends, you may not know that Normal people have this way of knowing when serious trouble is approaching.

BOOM!

The back door, which opens from the kitchen to the garden, groaned on its hinges as if someone had thrown themselves hard against it. All three jumped.

BOOM!

'Who's there?' Skelton said gruffly. He feared a gang of grey thugs, wanting to mash him to splinters.

Bonaparte's teeth gave an experimental *clack*, and began chattering.

Tibia squeezed himself in through the cat flap, ears first. 'Open the door! Hurry!' he said, speaking for the first time in a week. 'No time to explain.'

The back door shuddered again. And a volley of barking broke out.

'Open it? Are you sure?' asked Skelton.

'Do it!' said Tibia.

All fingers and pricking thumbs, Skelton started fumbling with the locks and chains. He opened the door a couple of inches, so that it was held only by one chain.

What Skelton saw was Grimsby, who lived with Skelton's Ordinary neighbour. But now the Normal dog's wide-eyed face was panting with fear.

'Hurry!' Grimsby shouted, thrusting his face into the opening door. A stone whizzed through the air to ricochet from the poor hound's rump. As he howled with pain, a drunken cheer went up from the neighbouring garden, and new stones, some of them quite big, pinged and whistled towards him.

'Hurry!' said Tibia, exasperated with Skelton's slowness. The last chain was unbelievably fiddly, but finally Grimsby barged into the room, blood in his short hair.

'Lock it, bolt it, bar it!' he panted. 'Hurry!'

Skelton slammed the door and quickly began to clunk shut the sliding bolts, and turn his skeleton key in the groaning wards of several locks. For the moment, he chose to ignore the fact that Grimsby, a guest, was ordering him about in his own home.

'What happened?' asked Bonaparte.

Before anyone could answer, an explosive *CRASH!* followed by an icy tinkle of glass came from the front room. Everyone fell silent. Nobody moved.

Fibula, the first to break the spell, darted away.

'A metal ball bearing! Between the bars of the front-room windows,' she said, her claws tapping on the wooden floor as she skittered back into the kitchen.

CRACK! CRACK! Stones bounced off the kitchen window, leaving a cobweb of splintered glass hanging in the frame.

Everyone started moving at once. They were on the edge of panic.

Please remain calm,' said Tibia steadily. 'Skelton... is this door bolted and chained as best you can make it?'

'Yes it is,' Skelton said.

'Bonaparte,' Tibia continued, 'please re-check the locks and chains on the front door.'

Bonaparte hurried off.

'Grimsby, old comrade: a reconnaissance mission. Go into the front room and have a good look out of the window. Report back with your findings.'

'Okay, General,' said Grimsby.

'General?' asked Skelton.

'Fibula my dear,' said Tibia quietly, would you mind running upstairs to let us know what you can see?'

Fibula sprang off.

'You are unexpectedly good in a crisis,' Skelton said to Tibia.

'Experience,' said Tibia mysteriously. 'Now, Skelton, from what I have just seen we are in for big trouble. We have to barricade the cat flap, and secure all the downstairs doors and windows.'

This being a Normal house, every door, inside and out, could be locked and bolted, while the windows had metal bars over them.

'Yes, I agree,' Skelton said stiffly. 'Although if anyone should be giving the orders... It should be the Master of Yawngrave Tower. In short: me.'

'Really?' said Tibia, raising an eyebrow. 'You?'

'Yes, *me*.' said Skelton.

But even Skelton knew there was no time for arguing. With bits of chain, a heavy wooden chair and a giant sack of dried rat spines, Skelton, Bonaparte and Tibia wedged the cat flap closed, and reinforced the back door.

Although there were no more stones cracking on the door for the moment, Skelton's thumbs assured him trouble was coming.

From the front room came a deep growling, and the sound of Grimsby bellowing out between the bars of the shattered window: 'I'll bite your heads off!'

'What we need, Skelton, is a council of war,' said Tibia.

Chapter 10

A Council of War

Tibia led the way, climbing upstairs to the Long Room on the first floor, where they took seats around Skelton's enormously long dining table, under the portraits of Skelton Kirkley Elvis Lionel Lupin Yawngrave I, and Skelton Kirkley Elvis Lionel Leroy Yawngrave II.

Grimsby barged in last of all, and scrambled into one of the chairs.

'The cheek of it,' he said.

'I agree,' Fibula said, 'those *rude* grey fools are everywhere.'

'Maniacal monochromers,' said Bonaparte.

'I would like to start,' said Skelton, 'by reminding people that Yawngrave Tower is *my* ancestral home...'

'Tower?' Grimsby asked.

Bonaparte rolled his eyes. For Skelton would always insist his home be called *Yawngrave Tower*, even though it plainly was just a perfectly Normal house in an everyday street.

'I'll agree, that to the uneducated eye' – here Skelton looked at everyone pointedly in turn –'my home appears to be a modest Normal dwelling. But tradition is tradition. As the Master of Yawngrave Tower it falls to *me* to declare this Council of War open.'

'Now, Skelton,' said Tibia. 'This is fighting business, and fighting business is what I know. I thought I had retired, but I was wrong. No offence was meant.'

Skelton nodded at Tibia in the way one gentleman nods at another. Tibia nodded back. Skelton returned the nod with extra courtesy. Tibia...

'That's right, General,' said Grimsby, interrupting the nodding. 'I followed you on fighting business when Mrs Bland got out of hand before, and I'll follow you again.'

'You did,' said Tibia, 'and I thank you. You have a loyal heart. Now Grimsby,' he went on gravely, 'please make your report.'

'It's bad, General,' said the dog. 'There were four or five of them on the street, all in grey. One was hefting half a brick from hand to hand, and eyeing the house as if he fancied chucking it at a window. He began to creep closer but I stuck my head out and barked. He almost wet himself. He scarpered back to his mates, all of them in those stupid grey clothes.'

'Well done, Grimsby,' said Tibia.

The Normal dog shook his head. 'I reckon they'll be back soon enough.'

'Fibula,' said Tibia, 'what did you see from upstairs?'

'Idiots spraying our fence again.'

Bonaparte groaned.

'One was on his phone and was clearly organising something,' Fibula continued, 'but even I couldn't hear what he was saying. Afterwards I saw six of them in Grimsby's garden. There's nothing stopping them from just climbing over to attack us. They've brought heavy sticks and big sacks. At the moment, though, they are drinking beer, and seem relaxed. It's like they are waiting for something.' Fibula paused. 'All I know is that I'm not going to end up in the river in one of those sacks.'

'Over my dead body, my dear,' said Tibia.

'What were those men doing in your garden, Grimsby?' Skelton asked.

'They came around this morning, making threats. One of them kept poking old Jim in the chest—'

'Your *owner*,' Skelton added nastily.

Grimsby ignored him. 'They kept asking Jim if I was a Normal dog, and saying that Normals weren't needed any more, and that all the trouble in the world was caused by *Normals*, and that goes for Normal dogs too.

'And after a while, Jim admitted I was Normal. He told them I had pretended to be an Ordinary dog, and tricked him into giving me a home, and free food and drink. Really, he said, I was a just con artist and a thief. I couldn't believe my ears,' Grimsby said sadly. 'I thought we were mates, Jim and me. When it came to it, he pretended he hardly knew me. But I don't know what they would have done to him, if he hadn't lied like that.

'Anyway, these blokes pushed Jim away, and ran at me. Old Jim just stood there. What else could he do? They had baseball bats and cricket bats. I think they actually wanted to kill me...'

'Go on Grimsby,' said Tibia.

'When they cornered me – lots of them, there were – I thought all I could do was to try to get few good bites in, before they did me in. Just then...' Grimsby cleared his throat. 'Just then my old comrade Tibia jumped from the fence at the head of one of the men. A distraction, it was. He held on with his legs wrapped around this horrible thug's head, and bit his ear till it bled.'

'That's right,' said Tibia.

'He didn't like it,' said Grimsby. 'Anyway, this was my chance. I'm no good at jumping, but I managed to dodge past the man Tibia was clawing, and break a hole in the fence where I'd been chewing it.'

'I *knew* it.' Skelton muttered.

'But Tibia sprang from the man's shoulders clean into Skelton's garden,' said Grimsby said. 'The thug was still waving his arms about in the air as Tibia sprinted up to the cat flap. The rest, all the stones and everything, you know.'

'These are not everyday Ordinary people,' said Bonaparte. 'These ones are openly wearing O.P.P. grey. They are the grey menace! Mrs Bland's brainwashed fanatics!'

'It seems,' Tibia said, 'we have no choice. We must fight to protect ourselves...'

'And Yawngrave Tower too,' said Skelton. 'And I am grateful to you all.'

'No need for gratitude, Skelton,' said Bonaparte grimly. 'There's no choice. We can't leave if we're surrounded.'

'We are at war, Skelton,' said Tibia. 'And we must fight back.'

With a sigh, Fibula consented to rub her fur against the second television in the corner of the Long Room. The static electricity this caused somehow sparked the TV into life. It was their only hope of getting any information. For some reason Skelton's phone and computer were not working. When Bonaparte tried to use his phone, he just heard a howling interference and his screen went dead. No messages of any sort could be sent either.

They cheered as the television flickered on. But the first thing they saw sickened them. Mrs Bland *was* the news. She was being interviewed standing in a London street.

'We are entirely fed up with Halloween,' she said. 'Why? Just think about it! It is a custom that celebrates evil things, and we've allowed it to go on far too long.'

Her supporters applauded, jostling behind her.

'Fortunately,' Mrs Bland continued, 'this year I have *persuaded* the Government to ban this evil festival. I am asking the people of this country to unite. Let's forbid trick-or-treating, or any of that evil nonsense. Imagine how proud the people of this great nation will be tonight knowing that this year instead of celebrating *unusual* behaviour, we can settle down to an Ordinary night with people quietly absorbed in their screens instead.

'This is not an attack on Normal people. I don't have anything against Normal people. It's just that the evil of Halloween shouldn't be allowed to continue.'

For a few seconds Skelton almost believed her, until he remembered what old Pop Yawngrave II used to say: the proof of the pudding is in the eating. And having your ancestral home surrounded by stone-throwing thugs with their bellies full of beer, and heads full of Mrs Bland's evil thoughts showed she was a liar. He switched off the television in disgust.

'Well,' he said. 'It is a good thing that this house is a Normal house. For, as everyone knows, they aren't the same as Ordinary ones. I think we have no choice. We must keep them at bay using some of the tricks and wheezes my brainy Yawngrave ancestors built into Yawngrave Tower over the centuries.'

'Well said, Skelton! What are they?' asked Fibula.

'Not sure yet,' Skelton said breezily. This was not the answer the others had hoped for, but Skelton pointed up to the oil paintings of his Yawngrave forefathers. 'I have never forgotten what Skelton Kirkley Elvis Lionel Lupus Yawngrave II said to me. "My lad," he said, "remember this: if the worst comes to the absolute and utter worst you have to go *upstairs*. But until that terrible moment... Never, *never* go there." So that's where I'll go: upstairs.'

'Upstairs?' said Fibula impatiently. 'There is no upstairs, Skelton. There's only a cramped attic full of I don't know what.'

'Sometimes,' Skelton said, walking over to the window and peering at the grey-clothed thugs drinking from beer cans in Grimsby's garden, 'you have to trust people. And I trust my distinguished father.'

'That's your plan? To go "upstairs", when Fibula the six-legged feline says there is nothing there?' said Bonaparte. 'We need a real plan. And fast! This is supposed to be a Council of War, not a Council of Hiding in the Attic.'

'Bonaparte,' Skelton said stiffly, 'please will you help me carry the portraits of my father and grandfather? I'm going upstairs.'

'You said *upstairs* again,' said Fibula, sounding quite tetchy.

'I did,' Skelton said gravely. 'Through the trapdoor. If there was ever a time to follow my father's advice, it is now.'

'We should go together,' said Tibia unexpectedly. 'Sometimes doing the unexpected in warfare can win you an advantage.'

'Just for your information,' said Grimsby from the window, 'Remember those men who were building bonfires? One's almost ready. They are pouring petrol on them. And yes... there it goes. It's alight.'

'And what will they want to burn on those fires? Penny for the Guy?' Bonaparte muttered.

'Let's get cracking, shall we?' Skelton said.

Chapter 11

The sinister staircase

Some of the most Normal things about Skelton's house were the unexplained noises. Many of them emanated from the attic that Skelton and his Normal friends were just about to explore. Skelton had often woken up sprawled on the floor, having been shocked awake by a wild racket somewhere above his room. It was one of the disadvantages of sleeping upright, hanging from comfortable sleeping hooks. While Bonaparte, who had been staying in the guest room since June, had spent hours listening to what sounded like a freshly murdered corpse being dragged about overhead.

Once in a multicoloured moon, whatever it was seemed to hold a boot-busting disco. Skelton could never quite catch the music, but the rhythmical, stumbling clump of dozens of feet enraged him. On such occasions, he hammered on the ceiling with a broom until it settled down.

But by morning, any desire to investigate always melted away with thoughts of breakfast. Occasionally an unexplained draught would surge down from the trapdoor in the hallway leading to the bathroom. It would catch Skelton in his slippers, making him yelp in surprise as goosebumps rose on his papery skin.

Now he was wobbling on a stepladder, under that very same trapdoor. His face was inches from the dark wood panelling of the ceiling. The trapdoor was just like the other panels but for one detail. It had a keyhole.

In the palm of his hand was his skeleton key, with an intricate eight-eyed spider-face design.

'Skelton, stop examining the stupid key, and use it!' cried Fibula. She and the others were all glaring up at him impatiently. Raucous shouts could be heard in the street, and some kind of lairy singing drifted up from the back garden.

'Skelton!' hissed Fibula.

'Trapdoor spiders are interesting,' said Bonaparte, who had been thoughtful for a while. 'They hold on to their trapdoors, and when something edible gets close they flip the doors open, and drag the victims down into their tunnels to be stored and slowly chewed or have the vital juices sucked out of them while they are still alive. Of course there would have to be an enormous spider to be holding on to a trapdoor this size, and naturally it would have to be upside down, but it's—'

'Bonaparte, will you shut up!' Skelton said.

Without even the tiniest comforting squeak, a square opened in the ceiling. Apprehensively, Skelton pushed his head into the lightless void.

Have you ever seen real darkness before? Not the kind you get in cities, with light filtering through the curtains, nor in the starlit countryside. This is a thick velvety blackness, that creeps and slithers nicely with interesting and unknown things. Normal people call it *the second kind of darkness*, and it is the blackest, most lightless experience you can imagine.

Luckily, most Normal people (except Bonaparte) feel very at home and relaxed in the second kind of darkness.

Skelton pulled himself into the black, and climbed slowly to his feet. He seemed to be standing on wooden floorboards, judging by the friendly creak they made as he shuffled forwards. He sneezed. Ancient dust had been disturbed, which now hung in the air. One by one his friends climbed up, through the square of dim light, to join him in the darkness. Bonaparte was last, precariously clutching the portraits of Skelton's father and grandfather. He left these a few paces from the trapdoor.

The trapdoor silently closed.

'We'll find our way out again, of course?'
Bonaparte asked, holding his hand centimetres in front
of his face. He could see nothing.

'Don't worry, lad,' said Grimsby. 'My nose works
in the dark.'

'Can you smell anything now?' asked Bonaparte.

'Oh yes.' They heard lips being licked. 'Bones.'

Grimsby and the cats wheezed with laughter.

Both Bonaparte and Skelton muttered something
about rudeness, and everybody began talking at once.

'Shhhh!' Skelton said. 'Stop it! Listen,' he said. *Stop
it! Listen,* came his echo. 'Everyone keep hold of
someone else, and I'll lead. It's bigger up here than we
think.'

'Before you do that, Skelton, old stick' Bonaparte
said, 'just listen for a minute more.'

'To what?' his friend asked. '*To what?*' whispered
the echo.

'Just listen,' said Bonaparte.

'I can't hear anything much,' Skelton said.

'Exactly,' said Bonaparte. That trapdoor seems to
have blocked every sound from outside. I don't like it.'

'Makes me wonder,' said Fibula, 'if there is an
outside any more.'

'What do you mean?' Bonaparte asked.

'Not sure,' she said, 'just that it feels very Normal in
here. Very Normal indeed.'

Bonaparte laughed nervously.

'But that's good isn't it?' Skelton soothed. 'We just have to keep calm. Bonaparte, try not to get rattled.'

Grimsby sniggered.

'It's only a bit of darkness,' Skelton said kindly, 'let's go.'

The fact that no one had brought a light might seem strange to Ordinary readers. These were Normal people, however, and the dark is a very Normal thing, and it never occurred to them to waste time hunting for a torch.

They arranged themselves in a line, Bonaparte's hand on Skelton's shoulder. Grimsby was sniffing at his ankle bones, which Bonaparte detested, while the two cats navigated by their whiskers. Skelton crept forward about twenty paces and stubbed his toe.

'Ouch!' he said, stopping abruptly and quickly sidestepping, which made everyone else bump into Bonaparte. 'Stairs,' he announced. 'Let's be careful now!'

'Stairs?' said Fibula. 'There shouldn't be stairs, just this attic.'

'I don't think we should go up those stairs,' said Bonaparte. 'Grimsby can you' – *clack* –'smell anything?'

'Not including present company,' Grimsby said, inhaling deeply, and sneezing. 'Dust, lots of it, dampness, and loads of bones.'

'*Not* including present company?' Skelton asked sternly.

'Yep, the smell comes from up here.'

Skelton climbed upstairs slowly. They seemed to be twisting leftwards, but at least they were Normal stairs, which complained loudly as they were stepped on. After about forty stairs, Fibula stopped everyone. 'I repeat. These steps make no sense. We should be right through the roof and snatching at sparrows by now,' she said. 'It's as big as, well as...'

'A Tower, Fibula?' said Skelton smugly. 'This is a Normal house, built by Normal people long ago. So anything can happen here.'

'Can anyone else see that?' Bonaparte said, sounding relieved. At the top of the stairs he thought he saw the faintest glow-worm glimmer.

'Yes,' said Tibia, 'if you mean that light.'

Having something to focus on, even if the light was tremendously faint, made climbing far easier. As they drew nearer, Fibula (who had exceptional vision) could see it more clearly. 'Picture a nice jug of pond water full of water fleas,' she told Skelton. 'Instead of drinking it down thirstily, you notice the fleas dancing about in it are tiny points of greenish light. Very odd.'

'Oh dear,' said Skelton.

'Not seen one of those for a long time,' said Tibia.

The light wasn't a light at all. It was a ghoul. It was doing all the things normal for a ghoul. For a start, it had a vague expression, like a face submerged under rippling, moonlit water. Its form was more like a suggestion of a human body than an actual body, but its phosphorescent jelly stood about the same height as Skelton. Nobody, however, could see any feet.

'As I live and breathe...' began the ghoul.

'That's rich,' said Grimsby.

'*Rudeness*,' said the ghoul in a surprisingly deep and fruity voice, as if he were a Shakespearian actor. 'As I was saying, as I live and breathe: it must be the third one. A bit early, aren't you?'

Nobody had ever called Skelton *the third one* except for his dear father. Although he was long dead, Skelton Yawngrave II still visited Skelton in dreams, shouting for him to get off his bed hooks, and get cracking off to school. On waking, Skelton would realise with relief that he no longer had to go to *Ye Normal School for Young Gentlefolk* or be caned on the backside for *rudeness* by Dr Barnabus Blunderbuss, the headmaster.

'Yes I am Three,' Skelton said.

'Three? You look terrible for your age,' wheezed Grimsby.

Skelton ignored him.

'I thought it was you,' said the ghoul, 'you're the spit of One and Two.'

111

'Thank you,' Skelton said sniffily. For he considered it impolite to say someone is the 'spit' of someone else. 'My noble father and grandfather,' he explained, 'were both exceedingly handsome gentlemen. In fact, people have often commented on how nice their faces were, especially their fine, deep-set eyes, and excellent teeth.'

'Yes, yes...' said the ghoul impatiently. 'Yes they do have a very individual style, if you're mad enough to like that kind of thing.'

Grimsby sniggered.

'But let me introduce myself,' the ghoul continued in a more Normal manner. 'My name is Spoony Pootus Olly Osgood Kooker, Warden of Yawngrave Tower. And it's nice to see you. And so many! Five is an excellent haul. So how was it? Not too painful I hope?'

'Was *what* painful?' Skelton asked.

'You know...' said Spoony Kooker.

'What do you *mean*?' Skelton asked, becoming irritated.

'Well, said the ghoul, 'I enjoy tales of how people, you know, died. I know it's a bit ghoulish, but then I can't really help that, can I?'

'Died?' Skelton said. 'Who has died?'

'You lot,' said the ghoul.

'But we didn't die,' said Skelton.

'So what are you doing here?' said the ghoul irritably. 'Why have you come to the third floor?'

'Third floor?' said Fibula. 'So the loft was the second floor, the Long Room and the bedrooms are on the first floor, and the kitchen is on the ground floor—'

'Excuse me, Fibula,' said Skelton. 'Listen, Spoony, it's because there's an emergency. The house is about to be attacked by an angry and very rude mob of Ordinary people, and Skelton Yawngrave II—'

'Two,' said Spoony Kooker.

'Skelton Kirkley Elvis Lionel Leroy Yawngrave II,' Skelton said pointedly, 'told me that in an absolute emergency, I should go upstairs.'

'Did he? Well you have succeeded. You're on the third floor now. You came up another flight of steps. All because a few Ordinary people got cross? You call that an emergency?'

'Yes I do,' Skelton said. 'I think they are going to try to burn the house down, and we need some extra special freakery to sort them out.'

'Why are those Ordinary people attacking you?' asked the ghoul. 'What have you done to them?'

'Nothing. It's all because Mrs Bland has come back,' Skelton said.

Spoony Kooker gave an extraordinary high-pitched shriek. 'I thought she was dead.'

'No. Sadly not,' said Tibia, wincing. His ears were still flat.

'What I find irritating, Mr Yawngrave,' said the ghoul, 'is that I have waited here for over fifty years for something to happen. And now you're telling me that you're not dead. And I suppose none of you lot are dead either?'

'Certainly not,' said Fibula.

'Blooming nerve,' said Grimsby.

The ghoul puffed out his cheeks.

'You see, if you've come this far you must continue. See that door over there?' The ghoul indicated a faint, blood-red patch in the absolute dark. 'It's full of answers.'

A chattering began a few inches away from Skelton's left ear. It was Bonaparte's teeth again.

'Skelton, I' – *clack* – 'I don't like the feel of that place at' – *clack* – 'all.'

'Not many people do,' said Spoony Kooker cheerfully. 'I'm told it smells bad too.'

Fibula swiped at the ghoul with a clawed paw. It went right through him.

'Well, I had to try,' she said to Tibia.

Eventually, the ghoul held up a hand. A death's-head hawkmoth flew out of the dark to him. It hovered a few centimetres above the ghoul's insubstantial palm. In Spoony's faint green glow, they could see the pattern of a little skull on the back of its furry thorax. As one of the most Normal of all moths, it was very beautiful. But it flew off again, dancing invisibly somewhere above their heads.

'I have thought of a compromise,' said Spoony Kooker. 'One of you must go through that door. The rest of you will wait here.'

'What's on the other side?' Skelton asked.

'It's for you to find out. But if you don't come back, I'll send in the other four, one by one.'

'Eyeballs to that,' said Grimsby. 'I'm off. I'm not waiting here to be sent anywhere by some smoky old spook. I'd rather take on the thugs.' He turned around and made to sprint down the stairs. But to his horror, the staircase had disappeared.

'You didn't think it would be so easy, did you?' Spoony Kooker asked. For once, Grimsby didn't answer back. Like the rest of them he could not drag his eyes from the blood-red patch in the darkness. The red door was making his neck bristle with fear.

'There's no' – *clack* – 'point in waiting Skelton, old' – *cl-clack* – 'chum,' said Bonaparte, pointing towards the door.

Skelton was just about to reply (and not very pleasantly), when the moth settled above his ear hole.

'Follow,' it whispered in a light and feathery voice, before burring away for a second. 'My name,' it whispered before alighting again by his right ear hole, 'is Diana. Anna. Indigo. Nocturna. Tremblina. Yellyface.'

Without speaking, Skelton followed the moth. His kneecaps twitching with fear.

'I didn't know moths had names,' he said, although they were one of the most Normal of the insects, and Skelton had eaten very few of them out of respect.

'But. We. Do,' Diana Yellyface whispered.

As Skelton followed the tiny creature, he wondered how it could form words. But asking that seemed to be disrespectful. Only once did he glance back at the others. They stood around the luminescent ghoul, and their eyes gleamed.

Perhaps, Skelton worried, his house was already full of invaders. What answers could be found here? Or would he die? Or would he be ambushed by monsters? A giant trapdoor spider perhaps…'

He felt a tickling on his cheek.

'Don't. Be. Afraid,' the death's-head hawkmoth whispered. This, of course, made Skelton feel worse. Eventually, from somewhere, he found enough courage to walk to the red and ominous door.

'Try. Not. To. Scream,' said the moth.

Chapter 12

The Red Room

Skelton stepped onto a smooth marble floor, as the
death's head hawkmoth burred around his head.
Although red light was falling from lamps hanging high
above, Skelton could not see a ceiling. The walls were
lined with tapestries, embellished with intricate designs.
These heavy cloths seemed to muffle his every creak or
footstep. Slowly, he walked between parallel rows of
raised stone plinths. There were nine on each side.

On top of each one were complete skeletons of
settled, dry bones. They had been placed, unnaturally
enough, on their backs. By each was a chiselled name.
Skelton paused halfway along to read SIR CARL
ANGUS REGIBALD YAWNGRAVE 1402–1623. His
face was fierce.

YAWNGRAVE!

Suddenly Skelton understood that he was walking
among the bodies of his ancestors.

He paused before the next Yawngrave. Under his feet were three or four saws and other mysterious and rusty instruments. QUARMUS UGO ARCHIBALD COLIN KIRKBODY YAWNGRAVE PhD. 1560–1709.

'Ah-ha!' Skelton whispered, 'the great surgeon.' He was drawn to walk past other plinths. Only one was unoccupied. It stood at the end of the second row.

SKELTON ELVIS LIONEL LUPUS YAWNGRAVE III 1894–

It was his name and his year of birth, but his date of death had not been engraved. Clearly he hadn't been expected. On the wall next to it was a tapestry. Unlike the others, this tapestry was incomplete. He squinted at it. There were dozens of intricate pictures of his life. There he was shrieking with happiness, being held upside down by the ankles and twirled in the air by his father. There he was as a schoolboy with Sunny Applebiter Dolmalus! The picture gave him a pang of pain. There he was with Bonaparte eating pies. And there… A great wall of flame! And beyond that nothing. The pattern ended.

A rustle came from behind him. Something was stirring. On the plinth opposite his own, one of the skeletal figures had squeaked up onto one elbow. It yawned.

'Is that you, my boy?'

That voice! It was his own dear father.

'Pop,' Skelton stammered out. 'Is that you?'

'It is, you young splinter.'

'Pop is this where you live now?'

'*Live?* You never were the sharpest dagger in the dark,' said Skelton's father with a sigh.

'So you're still...' Skelton was confused.

'Dead as a doornail. Of course I am,' his father said. 'You came to my funeral and ate eighty-two triangular maggot-and-toadstool sandwiches to assuage your grief. Ah,' he went on wistfully, his mind wandering for a moment, 'a good old-fashioned maggot-and-toadstool sammige... Still, it was a good do, as I remember it; a fitting send-off. Dancing! And the people so colourfully dressed. But you, young Skelton,' his father continued with sudden concern in his voice, 'surely you're not ready to join us yet? Not in those clothes! Average at best. You can't have come from your funeral.'

'No Pops, I didn't.'

'So why are you here? A spot of grave-robbing perhaps? A bold move, my boy.'

'No, Pops,' Skelton said, 'I arrived here randomly, my dear old cudgel.'

'I don't believe in random! Only you could stumble into the afterlife by accident,' he said affectionately. 'So you'll have met Spoony Kooker?'

'Yes,' Skelton said.

'Annoying, isn't he? He likes a bit of drama.'

It was so good to see his father, and there were a million things Skelton had wanted to ask the old man over the years. But now he couldn't think of one. 'It is really good to see you Pop,' he said.

'You too, m'boy,' his father said, yawning. 'The problem is that when you're up here you spend most of the time, um, resting. Is it almost Halloween?'

'Tonight,' said Skelton.

'Ah! No wonder I was feeling frisky. But we all fancy a bit of a knees-up this time of year, don't we? Even right back to old Skolbard Yawngraef over there,' he said, pointing at the oldest plinth of all.

Were Skelton's eyes playing tricks? One of Skolbard's fingers had seemed to twitch.

'Even he gets up for a bit of a dance at Halloween. Tradition, isn't it? Although,' his father added quietly, 'he capers about holding a great heavy axe, which I can tell you smarts nastily if he catches your shin with it.'

'Anyway Pops, you're right. It is tradition. Except in the world downstairs, Mrs Bland is planning to ban Halloween, and fun, and tricks and treats. In fact, I think she is trying to ban Normal people.'

'Ban Normal people? How can she? I forget things,' said Pop, 'how long do Ordinary people live again?'

'Not very long,' Skelton said. 'Poor things. Only to about a hundred I suppose, and that's if they're lucky.'

'The thing is, I remember Mrs Bland from when I was *downstairs*. I think she's about the same age as you. What's that now, over a hundred?'

'Well over,' said Skelton.

'Anyway, I have never thought she was as Ordinary as she makes out. Hum...' said Skelton's father, 'Hum...'

'Pops. A big gang of Mrs Bland's people are about to attack Yawngrave Tower...'

'What?!?' Skelton's father sat bolt upright. 'Why didn't you say something before? You really take the biscuit sometimes. No concentration, always being distracted, always listening to the radio and dancing instead of doing your homework... Now. What was I saying again?'

'You were going to tell me what to do about the thugs attacking Yawngrave Tower,' said Skelton calmly, 'and probably setting fire to it right now and everything.'

'Of course. So here's what you do. Listening? Good. Here we go then. Number one: get past the ghoul. Number two: get downstairs onto the second floor, the extra dark bit, find the big lever, and yank it. Think you can remember that, you young creaker?'

'Will it help?' asked Skelton.

'A few years before you rattled your way into the world m'boy, I yanked that lever. Very lively. Very lively indeed. And very helpful. There comes a time in every Yawngrave's life when he must pull the lever. Gives you a fighting chance.'

'Great!' Skelton said. 'I've got to go. One: get past the ghoul. Two: yank the lever.'

'Listen, you ivory-headed loafer,' his father continued, '*this is very important*. To defeat Mrs Bland you need the help of Ordinary people too. Normal people can't do this on their own. Fighting Mrs Bland takes everyone. Do you understand?'

Skelton nodded firmly. As he did so, he felt the lightest touch on his cheek, and the moth fluttered between them.

'Time. To. Go,' she burred.

Skelton's father yawned, suddenly very sleepy indeed after the effort of talking to his son.

'Just use your brains, best of boys,' he said faintly, for his head was sliding back on its uncomfortable pillow, like an Ordinary person. Just as it seemed he was asleep, Skelton's father gave a start, and held his hand out.

'Oh! There's this, I almost...' He opened his hand, and in it was a pin with a small triangular head, with a design of interwoven knots.

'Take it,' whispered the moth.

Respectfully Skelton slid the object from his father's hand. For his father was immobile again.

Skelton, it is destined for you.
Rightfully, this thing is yours.
With it you make progress.

Skelton spun around. Women's voices? But where had they come from? There was nothing in the red gloom other than the rows of his dead ancestors.

'Did you hear them?' Skelton said.

'Who?' Diana fluttered in his ear.

'Women's voices?'

'No. In. Your. Head. Come on. Time. To. Go,' she whispered.

'I understand that we must go, you skull-sporting lepidopteron, but... but...' A great longing to stay in the most Yawngravey place in the whole world gripped Skelton. A deep snooze with his father seemed much easier than bothering with the horror downstairs. His eyelids drooped and his head grew full of pillowy thoughts. He decided to rest his head on the corner of his father's plinth for a moment.

Skelton! Do not sleep!
Wake up!
Do not drift into death!

Again! Women's voices in his head.

Skelton felt something alight on his temple.

'No!' urged the moth. 'Danger! Danger! It's. Not. Your. Time.'

Skelton snapped awake, panicked.

Staying in the Red Room was all wrong. He scrambled to his feet and sprinted, the moth trailing behind him in the air.

Chapter 13

A call to arms

Skelton galloped from the Red Room only to find the spectral Warden flapping angrily at his friends.

'So,' Grimsby was saying, 'are you a gas Kooker or an electric Kooker?'

'I don't endure the centuries to listen to *this*,' said the ghoul.

'Spoony,' Skelton said. 'Let's go. I have asked my father what to do, and he told me. There are deeds to be done.'

'Ah,' said the ghoul. 'Deeds, eh? If only it were as simple as that. There are rules.'

'Rules? I make the rules here,' said Skelton. 'We need to go down to the second floor. I need to pull a lever.'

The phantom flicked at him. 'Perhaps, being a Yawngrave, you can walk free,' he said. 'The others must stay.'

'No way,' said Grimsby.

'If I could bite you, Kooker, know that I would,' said Tibia.

'But you can't, can you? You cantankerous feline,' replied Spoony, darting about Tibia's battered head.

Everyone was getting cross. The Warden folded his insubstantial arms and turned away.

Diana Yellyface alighted on Skelton's head.

'I'll. Come. With. You,' she whispered, her voice just loud enough for the ghoul to hear.

'But you can't leave me to take care of all those knobbly old snoozers alone,' Spoony said, hanging in the air like a dead eel. 'It's only once every hundred years or so that one creeps upstairs, and that's it. This one has years in him yet. Barring accidents, of course,' he added more brightly.

'No,' said the moth. 'We're. Friends. But. Sometimes. You give. Me. A pain. Where. My. Head. Meets. My. Thorax.'

'You give her a pain in the neck, Kooker' said Bonaparte helpfully, 'and she's not the only one.'

The long silence that followed was interspersed with people tutting.

'Okay,' said the ghoul, suddenly. 'I'll let you out. See, Diana? I made the stairs come back again.' The moth drifted towards him in the air.

'Well done, Spoony,' Skelton said, turning to the others. 'I vote we bring him downstairs.'

'Are you mad?' said Bonaparte. 'This rag on a stick Kooker *seriously* gets on my nerves.'

'Having a ghoul with us could be useful,' said Skelton.

'Take me with you? A holiday? Yes please!' said Spoony Kooker growing soft and rounded as a cloud.

'Okay,' said Skelton, 'you can come downstairs. Please try to be helpful.'

'Instead of being infuriating,' added Bonaparte, 'which is what you are.' This was a bit unfair. The faint greenish light Spoony emitted had definitely helped Bonaparte to feel braver about the dark.

'The second floor,' the ghoul announced helpfully.

Nothing about the layout of the second floor made sense. Fibula had always thought it was just a loft, whatever claims Skelton had made for it. But the loft appeared to be at least three times bigger than the floors Skelton lived in below, just as the Red Room somewhere up above had seemed enormous. Soon the ghoul and the moth were hovering over an immense lever protruding from the floor.

'Could this be what my Pop was talking about?' Skelton cried.

'What does it say high up on the wall?' asked Fibula.

Long ago, a brass plaque had been screwed into a wooden roof beam. On tiptoe Skelton read it aloud thanks to the ghoul's faint glow:

THIS ONE STUPID

'Are you sure this is the right one?' said Bonaparte.

'Pops wouldn't let me down,' said Skelton.

'But...' began Bonaparte. But Skelton had already seized the lever by its brass handle, and had pulled it down hard.

Nothing happened.

Then *something* happened.

Incredibly Normal sounds filled the air. Great beams of wood were being forced to splinter and snap and fall with a great *thunk!* into place. Enormous doomy booming noises echoed about the room, followed by the clash and din of hammered sheets of metal. The house was convulsing. The thin men's jaws rattled, as the floor shook and rumbled. With a jerk, sections of the floor began to revolve in mystifying circles, while floorboards began to slide back revealing inky depths below, or entire room-sized sections shifted and moved aside.

Those who were not airborne, leapt from one sliding surface to another, or wobbled like they were on careering skateboards. Two or three times the floor split open dangerously, disclosing a deep vault stuffed with stores and provisions of all kinds. Bonaparte, yelping in alarm, teetered on the brink of one that bristled with sharp blades, till Grimsby clamped his teeth on the hem of his jacket and dragged him to safety.

Walls tore and split to allow light to stream through. The friends had been so long in the dark that even though it was cloudy, and the sun had almost set, they had to squint. Dark corners sprouted hundreds of flickering candles. Bedazzled for a moment, Diana blundered dangerously towards a flame. Fibula deftly caught her (with claws politely sheathed), until she steadied herself.

Panting, Skelton and Bonaparte saw sunken chambers were opening up around them, containing barrels, and bulky packages of food and provisions. Enough to survive a siege. Descending ladders to reach these treasures were everywhere.

Skelton rushed to peer from the new windows. They were like the slits in old castle walls, called loopholes, through which his ancestors might have fired arrows. The front garden seemed far away and, much of it was immediately beneath him. Peering upwards, Skelton saw his house was spreading out into the sky, with branches of castle turrets.

'Now do you believe me?' Skelton was dancing a rather snake-hipped Charleston, a popular dance when he was a young man. 'I live in a Tower, I always knew it!'

The others had too much to see, however, to listen to Skelton's crowing.

'Weapons!' said Tibia, pointing excitedly into a deep vault. It was lined with racks of ancient pikes, swords, rattling chains, bows and arrows, blunderbusses, daggers, dirks, bludgeons and cudgels.

They found another brass plaque when they climbed down the ladders.

> EMERGENCY USE ONLY
> **FIGHTING IS THE LAST RESORT.**

As Tibia was telling them the names of all the weapons, another deep rumble shook the Tower. It was as if a giant was clearing its throat.

The summons began.

It started as little more than a faint ringing in their ears, but even this made Skelton and Bonaparte feel trembly and full of vibrations. Tibia, Fibula and Grimsby sprang about with their ears pricked up as the signal became louder and deeper. Now Bonaparte and Skelton could hear it clearly, if 'clearly' is the word. It was like trumpets, choirs, huge drums, sitars, bagpipes, dusty church organs, electric guitars, crashing cymbals, bass notes, mad jazzy saxophones, as well as the calls of birds and animals and the sound of old windmills all mixed into one spine-tingling experience. But this description does it no justice.

The ghoul, rippling with colour, began to zip excitedly from corner to corner, bouncing on the ceiling and dipping in and out of the newly opened vaults in the floor. He shouted, 'It's a summons! It's a summons!' Diana Yellyface flapped joyfully after him. Together they made an amazing aerobatic display.

The wild and mysterious blast seemed to mean something different to all of them. Skelton felt strong and proud of his house. He thought of his father. Bonaparte stopped fiddling with his torn jacket, smiled and began muttering, *well I never*, to himself in a frisky voice. Tibia stood up straight and wiped a tear from his eye, like a proud old soldier at a remembrance parade. Grimsby, rolled on his back like a puppy, and Fibula danced with an expression of fiercely loving joy.

How the summons from Yawngrave Tower affected people, was a private matter. But if you were Normal, it seemed to do you the power of good.

Far away the sound reached the grounds of Charcoal House, inspiring Rick at this very moment to swoop bravely into the flames to rescue Grace Brown.

Some of the O.P.P. members had fled in dismay when Skelton's Normal house became a Tower.

Others, however, were emboldened. The transformation filled a few of the grey clad people with bitterness and hate. Their prejudices were confirmed: here was another example of Normal trickery.

They gathered in safety a small distance away, muttering. If these Normals wanted to seem like fake conjurors, and silly magicians, so be it. For what did you do to witches and wizards?

Burn them.

So they busied themselves building fires, stopping from time to time to stare in resentful wonder at the Tower. It was growing like a big spreading tree, branching weird turrets metre by metre into the sky.

As the night wore on, did any of the men below notice the erratic course of something big, with bat-like wings, tumbling from the sky towards the tallest turret?

No. They had more evil work to do. One of the O.P.P., a large man with a tattooed head, picked up a bottle with a strip of rag poking out of it. Carefully, he lit the rag with a cigarette lighter, and hurled the bottle at the Normal's disgusting building.

He had aimed well. The bottle smashed against the front door. It contained petrol, and the burning fuel began to lick hungrily at the wood.

Another bottle crashed onto the window frames.

The fire had started.

Chapter 14

Intruders

So this is the point where two threads of our story weave together.

Escaping from Charcoal House, Grace and Rick have just landed on the top of Yawngrave Tower, which had magically forked into high turrets that branched and spread like a vast tree.

After the extraordinary music of the summons, Skelton had begun a rapid, but triumphant exploration of his home. He galloped up the brand new spiral staircase of the tallest turret, with Bonaparte and Fibula hot on his heels, to reach yet another trapdoor. This popped open when Skelton barged upwards with his shoulder. He and Bonaparte emerged onto a windy, slightly swaying platform high above the street only to find two exhausted children.

One was Grace Brown, the other was Rick. But when Bonaparte heard who Rick's mother was, the trouble started.

'Stop it!' Skelton yelled at Bonaparte, who had taken a fistful of Rick's hair and with the intention of dashing the bat boy's head open. 'Bonaparte! You toothache, let him go! What are you thinking? He's Normal! We summoned him here.'

'He's a spy!' said Bonaparte, still holding onto Rick's hair, and jerking the boy's head towards Skelton. 'Just look at his spying face! And,' he said, pointing at Grace with his free hand, 'she's been brainwashed like the others.'

'His face *is* a spying face,' said Fibula, who had only just sped out of the trapdoor.

'I have *not* been brainwashed, Mr Bonaparte,' said Grace 'So please let him go! It's not Rick's fault that woman is his mother.'

'Listen to her, Bonaparte,' Skelton said.

Slowly, and with obvious reluctance, Bonaparte released his grip. Rick stood up warily, glowering at them.

'I came here because I followed the sound, you idiot,' he said.

'That's right,' said Grace. 'Mrs Bland was going to delete me, and Rick saved my life.'

'Delete you?' Skelton sounded shocked. 'There's a lot to discuss here—' he began.

Fibula sprang onto his shoulder. 'Stop discussing things, you old creaker! Bring these children downstairs and do something about the FIRE at the front door!'

'The fire! Of course.' He rushed to the side and saw the appalling sight of the blaze at his front door. 'Follow me!' Skelton hurtled back to the trapdoor and jumped through it, rapidly followed by Bonaparte and Fibula. Grace followed, but stopped as she saw it led to a staircase spiralling downwards.

'Wait!' said Rick. 'I didn't fly all the way here to take orders from *them*. What was I thinking? They're idiots.'

'But you were drawn here, weren't you? There must be a reason,' said Grace. 'And where else could you go?'

'How should I know?' Rick sounded angry. 'Anywhere. France maybe. I bet I could fly there from here.'

'Well I'm going with them,' said Grace. 'I met them once before, and they were kind and polite.' The thin men had already clattered out of sight, so Grace clambered through the trapdoor, and began to run down the narrow stairs, which had no handrail. She flitted between patches of candlelight. The flames guttered noisily and sent black smuts into the air as she passed.

Someone was climbing back up the stairs towards her.

It was Skelton.

'Grace Brown!' he said, 'I just wanted to say that having you with us is really important. You see, I was talking to my dead father, earlier…'

'Your dead father?' said Grace, slowly.

'And he said I needed to work with Ordinary people to fight Mrs Bland. I think you are one of the Ordinary people he meant.'

'I'll try to be,' said Grace. 'I hate Mrs Bland too. She wanted to burn me.'

'Burn you? Why?'

'She said I was a witch,' said Grace.

'Did she now?' said Skelton, looking hard at her.

'Yes,' said Grace. 'I think she is mad. Anyway, Rick saved me—'

'Do you need to work with me too, Yawngrave?' interrupted Rick sourly, from behind Grace. He had come down the spiral stairs too.

'Now Rick I know we didn't get off to the best of starts,' said Skelton. 'I apologise for Bonaparte. It's no excuse, but we have all been under a lot of stress. A siege no less! But, being who you are, I believe you must have an important story.'

Six paws' worth of claws rattled towards them.

'Hurry UP!' growled Fibula. 'Skelton, we need help below!'

When they emerged from the spiral staircase into light, Grace did not know what to look at first. If her magnifying glass had still been in her pocket, she could spend a week making detailed observations. The walls were supple and damp, and seemed to be made of living wood. Here and there the room she was in gaped open to form rounded chambers, or branched upwards to create new turrets above, or opened into sunken spaces bristling with ancient swords and shields.

With his heart thumping, only then did Skelton fully realise the extent of the transformation. They were in the old loft, but the trapdoor was gone. Instead there was a wide flight of stairs leading down past his bedrooms and the Long Room, all the way down to the ground floor.

This was Grace's first sight of the Tower's other inhabitants. There was the six-legged cat she had encountered on the top of the Tower. Fibula was peering from the long thin windows at the back. Grace could not decide if the cat's movements were so fluid and graceful because of her extra legs, or despite them.

Near Fibula was a dog who she soon learnt was called Grimsby. As soon as he opened his mouth, and began talking she knew he was Normal too. He appeared blocky and strong. He seemed to be organising the protection of the front of the house.

In the centre of the room was another Normal cat with magnificently scarred and battered ears. It was deep in thought as they arrived, pushing little metal soldiers around on a map of the street spread across a trestle table.

Tibia looked at Skelton, full of concern.

'Are you saying that the magnificent call of Yawngrave Tower has managed to summon just two children to add to our force?'

'For now,' said Skelton. 'But two children are better than none, Tibia.'

'I was hoping for an army,' sighed Tibia.

'Even if other Normal people wanted to come,' said Grimsby, 'they'd have to fight through all this lot outside.'

Tibia agreed.

'You have to forgive my rudeness. You are very welcome,' Tibia said to the children. 'We have been very busy putting out a fire at the front door,' he said pointedly.

'Thank goodness! I knew it wouldn't be a problem,' said Skelton.

'Humph,' said the ghoul from the corner of the room, glowering at the Master of Yawngrave Tower.

While Grace had seen Normal people and animals, she had never seen anybody like Spoony Kooker, who until now had been hanging motionlessly in the air, his body the rusty colour of a stagnant pond in autumn.

She did not notice Diana at all. It was only when she followed Rick's eyes that she saw the moth, settled flat against the wall. She went to stand next to Diana, who burred a welcome in her tiny voice.

Meanwhile Grimsby and Bonaparte trundled a swinging brass bucket on miniature train tracks. The bucket approached a hole in the floor. Because the building had mysteriously changed shape, becoming wider the higher up you went, Grimsby was now standing over the garden below. Squinting down through the opening in the floor, Grimsby had been able to douse the flames from above. Now he turned his attention to the thugs. Grace had been too polite to ask where the smell of rotting fish heads came from, but now she realised it came from the spewy goo that the Normal dog, taking careful aim, slopped out to splatter onto the heads below. Usefully, it made the front garden and its path more slippery than ice.

'Bulls-eye!' Grimsby shouted, watching a thug get drenched in it, and slide off his feet into the gloop.

But Grimsby's triumphant shout was cut short.

'They're attacking the kitchen!' shrieked Fibula, peering through one of the Tower's loopholes into the back garden. One of them has a sledgehammer, and there's one with an axe!'

Immediately, there was a thud on the back door downstairs, followed by an ominous splintering. They all listened in horror as the sound of a thick steel blade crunched onto wood two, then three more times.

Wasting no time, Skelton decided to arm himself.

He hurried down a ladder into the armoury, and spidered back up moments later with a curved cutlass clamped between his teeth. Grace ducked, and everyone – even Spoony Kooker – took cover as his blade whistled in the air.

'Watch that blooming sword,' yelled Grimsby.

'It's a cutlass,' said Skelton, taking a moment to admire the curved blade's design of interlocking mer-spiders. 'Nobody invades Yawngrave Tower without a fight!' he shouted.

Without a second's thought, he skipped downstairs, taking two or three steps at a go, waving the piratical blade as he went.

Diana Yellyface came burring after him, narrowly evading the flailing blade. 'Wait! Stupid!' she said in Skelton's ear.

'What?' asked Skelton, stopping. 'Before doing battle with rapscallions, I get *rudeness* from a moth?'

'Another. Lever,' burred the death's-head hawkmoth.

140

'*Another* lever?' Skelton repeated.

'Yes.' said Diana. 'The house is growing. New things. All. The. Time. Another. Lever!'

Skelton turned around to face the others who, although they had kept a safe distance from the cutlass, were right behind him. Many of them had bared their teeth, and were looking rather fierce.

Not knowing what to do, Grace had also followed. But Rick hung back, his wings wrapped about him like a black cloak.

'With me!' said Diana Yellyface, and Skelton leapt back after her. Tutting, the others retreated too, despite the increasing urgency of the splintering from the kitchen.

Diana led Skelton to a new lever, which must have just recently emerged from an aperture in the wall. In the hollow this formed was another brass plaque:

TO OPERATE INTRUDER REPELLER:

1) *Grasp lever in your hands.*
2) *Pull it! You young air-brained rattler.*
3) *Locate umbrella (optional).*

Yr. affectionate father
Skelton Yawngrave II

Everyone crowded around the new lever.

'Signed by my father,' said Skelton. 'What do you think it means?'

From below, there was a cacophony of crunching wood, and the sound of boots on broken glass. A triumphant chanting broke out. *O.P.P.! O.P.P.! O.P.P.!*

Was that the smell of burning?

'Just pull the flipping thing, can't you?' Grimsby barked in fear.

After glaring at Grimsby for his *rudeness*, Skelton began to pull hard on the huge lever.

O.P.P.! O.P.P.! Came the chants.

Grimsby flung himself at the metal rod that Skelton was evidently struggling with.

THUNK! The lever had given.

The walls of the War Room began steaming like a wet pavement in the sun. But it was an extremely Normal steam, concentrating quickly into a dense cloud that hid the ceiling. More fog was rolling down out of the spiral staircases.

From the wet mass a cloudy dark tentacle probed its way out, passing clean through Spoony Kooker (who shuddered). Rick stepped aside from it, but it patted the top of Bonaparte's head, leaving a crown of dewy beads on his skull.

At the top of the stairway, it stopped. It met a thin stream of smoke, rising suddenly from some new fire inside the house. The dark tentacle quivered in response and, like a river of leaden cloud, it flowed downstairs.

Chapter 15

Time to fight

'Let's follow this mysterious cloud,' Skelton bellowed, brandishing his cutlass.

But Tibia, Fibula, Grimsby and Bonaparte had already charged downstairs without waiting for him. With a belated bellowing cry, he set off to join his comrades.

It seemed that Grace and Rick had been left behind.

'I think we should go too,' Grace said.

Rick shrugged, hanging back. 'Yeah,' he said. 'Maybe.'

Meanwhile, Skelton had blundered into Bonaparte at the bottom of the stairs. He had armed himself with a spear in addition to the cutlass, and was now pointing its tip towards the kitchen, which sounded as if it were full of men shouting with aggressive laughter.

With his head in the cloud, it was impossible to see. Skelton found it was only a metre thick, so when he reached the foot of the stair, he and stepped into the hallway and ducked down... There! He saw them.

There were seven strangers crowded in the kitchen. Big men who stank of beer, and rotten fish courtesy of the spewy stuff that Grimsby had rained down on the Tower's besiegers.

Skelton's knees trembled. Tibia, however, seemed very poised, and this helped calm him. For the general's battle-scarred face made anyone who saw him feel a bit braver. Perhaps that's why they had all locked their eyes on the cat.

Tibia smiled back in an unconcerned way as the thugs laughed at him contemptuously. He liked being underestimated in times of trouble. He had moved his troops to different spots with significant nods and paw movements like a football coach.

'Wait!' he said to Skelton, who he could tell had been thinking of rushing the men. 'Let them make their first mistake. Stand with Bonaparte on the stairs for now. We'll respond if they advance.'

For once Skelton did as asked. He squatted just beneath the cloud line, next to Bonaparte on the stairs.

One of the thugs must have set one of the gold-coloured sofas in the front room on fire. Smoke was billowing out from the open door and mixing uneasily with the cloud. Skelton noticed grimy wisps of cloud probing out through the letterbox, as if tempted outside. The dirty smog smeared the tops of their shiny heads, and dribbled unpleasantly down their collars.

'Is this what they call the fog of war?' said Skelton.

Bonaparte shrugged, not trusting himself to speak in case his teeth chattered.

At a signal from Tibia, Spoony Kooker and the Normal death's-head hawkmoth Diana Yellyface began to dip in and out of the cloud.

'We've called the police!' Bonaparte shouted down at the thugs, shaking his skinny fist. The truth was different. None of their phones had worked for over a day now.

Worse, the intruders seemed to know it.

'The police? You little liar,' said one voice.

The gang laughed nastily. 'We'll deal with you when we're ready, bone boy.'

There was more raucous hooting. Two more cans were ripped open, and beer slopped onto the sticky floor.

Bravely, Diana Yellyface flitted into the kitchen. One of the thugs lunged at her, spilling his drink.

On the stairs, Rick suddenly pushed between Skelton and Bonaparte, vaulting over the hand rail into the fog. When he dropped out of it again, he was standing alone in the hallway, staring at the intruders. His great bat wings unfurled.

'Do you know me?' he growled at the men.

Choked with laughter, one hooligan sprayed a mouthful of beer over his comrades. Staggering drunkenly, he very carefully put down his can on the floor (flashing his O.P.P. tattoo on his shaven scalp) and selected half a brick from a pile the men had brought in.

He swaggered forward.

'I hate Normals,' he said to Rick. 'Why would I know a freakshow like you?'

The other thugs did not laugh this time. Skelton could smell violence in the air. It was even stronger than Bonaparte's favourite aftershave, *Le Squelette Pour Homme*.

Skelton noticed, with a twinge of fear in his stomach, that two of the men had baseball bats. Another had a fire axe.

'Do you know me?' said the boy again. His voice was imperious.

'He's Mrs Bland's son all right,' muttered Bonaparte into Skelton's earhole. He was impressed, despite himself, at the boy's raw courage.

Grace arrived too. She paused between the two skeleton men, holding a bag of small metal ball bearings.

In a heartbeat, she skipped down and stood with Rick.

'No, Grace!' Skelton shouted, now even more fearful. Tibia was beckoning her furiously. But Grace was on her own mission. She slammed the door of the front room to keep the smoke in, wondering why no one had done this before.

'Get out,' she shouted to the louts in the kitchen.

The man with the O.P.P. tattoo viciously threw the brick at Grace.

Instantly Rick reacted. He struck out with his foot, deflecting the lump in mid-air. It bounced from the wall close to Grace's head.

'I'll tell you who I am,' he said. 'I am Rick Bland, your beloved leader's son.'

'You freaking liar.'

The intruders had waited long enough. Tightly bunched, they began to advance.

'Hold!' Tibia ordered.

The cloud started raining. Hard. It pinged off the tops of the men's heads, and it bedraggled the cats. The hiss of steam came from the front room.

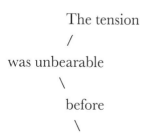

The tension
/
was unbearable
\
before
\

a blinding

\

white

\

FLASH

/

stabbed

/

death

\

from above!

Thunder exploded. Everyone was knocked from their feet. Above their heads, Yawngrave Tower resonated like a vast drum, whose rumble sounded across London.

Picking herself up from the floor, Grace noticed the air smelling of sweet ozone. Her companions stumbled to their feet, full of wonder.

'Ah-ha!' Skelton yelled. 'The intruder repeller. How exceptionally Normal.'

Painfully, the thugs picked themselves from the floor.

'Where's Tommo?' one said.

Wide-eyed, another pointed to the floor where there was an oily spot among the sparkle of broken glass. A wisp of smoke trailed up from the mortal remains of man with the O.P.P. tattoo.

This should have scared them away. Instead, it maddened them. They charged.

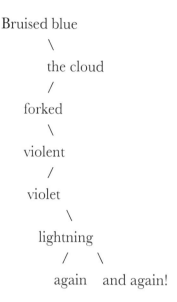

Bruised blue
    \
   the cloud
   /
  forked
   \
  violent
   /
  violet
    \
   lightning
   /   \
   again and again!

Two more oily stains on the floor.

There were only four invaders left now.

'The cloud,' said Rick, his wings outstretched, 'is deleting you! Leave now! Save yourselves.'

Most people, Ordinary or Normal, would have run away. But their eyes were robotic. The ringleader was a huge man with **BLAND** tattooed on his forehead.

Undaunted, he strode forward swinging a heavy baseball bat.

'Come on lads!' he shouted. 'Let's get stuck in. Look at them! Filth! They're disgusting...'

Another signal from Tibia.

Bonaparte, leaning from the stairs, stabbed down with his spear. The leader caught hold of its shaft. He dragged Bonaparte, grimly holding the spear, over the banisters. His fist swung and dealt Bonaparte a glancing blow to his face.

'Have that, bone boy!' he screamed.

'Careful with that cutlass!' Tibia shouted.

Skelton charged, wildly whistling the blade over his head. It would have nastily sliced Spoony Kooker, a flapping battle flag below the cloud, if the ghoul had been more substantial.

The bruiser wavered. Skelton, closing his eyes, thrust his blade towards him. The cutlass seemed to have other ideas. It slipped from his hand at the crucial moment, to embed its point in the wood of the ceiling. It was stuck firm.

'Now!' Tibia shouted.

The thug swung his baseball bat at Skelton, who ducked at the last moment.

Tibia, Grimsby and Fibula sprang. They dealt out ferocious lacerations on the man's legs. Fifty cat claws and three sets of exceedingly snappy mouths shredded his clothes and drew blood in several places.

'Argh!' roared the man, dancing in agony. 'Get them off me!'

Bonaparte grabbed the man's hand (the letters **h a t e** tattooed across his knuckles) and bit him. As Skelton observed later, if you considered how many pies that gannet-faced creaker chomped through in a day, nobody would doubt his jaw strength.

The thug's eyes bulged with pain.

At that second, something wonderfully decisive and totally Yawngraveish happened.

Almost as if the ceiling had violently spat it out, Skelton's cutlass landed hilt first on the thug's head. It bounced off, leaving the man knocked senseless on the floor.

'Did you see that?' Skelton said, waving his arms about in joy. 'I name you *The Skullcruncher*,' he said stooping down to reclaim the blade.

'No you don't,' said Tibia. 'You could have hurt someone with that.'

'That's the idea, isn't it?' said Skelton.

'Yes but you stand more chance of slicing one of us with it than anyone else,' said Tibia. 'Put it down.'

'Yes, do as you're told, you prancing popinjay,' said Bonaparte.

Reluctantly Skelton laid *The Skullcruncher* aside.

'Watch out!' said Grace, pointing, as two of the other thugs again hurtled forwards.

'Wings!' shouted Tibia.

Diana Yellyface fluttered around the men's heads to distract them.

Grace rolled a handful of metal balls under their feet, causing the men to slide. One man fell over. Rick rose up on his bat wings and swooped. The men flinched and tried to grab his legs as he passed. But instead they found Spoony Kooker's face, made giant and embellished with many sharp fangs, squeezing horribly between them.

Rick banked away in the tightly confined space. He disappeared momentarily into the cloud, as the fighting broke out. He returned, with a strangely satisfied expression on his face, kicking wildly at the arms below.

This was the crucial moment in the battle. The air was full of fists and wings, and smoke and cloud and a screeching ghost. Underneath was a field of teeth and claws and clubs and steel and the metal balls Grace was scattering underfoot.

The rain continued to fall, and still the thugs advanced down the hallway.

One of them booted Grimsby really hard, and the poor dog whimpered with pain, but before he could get another kick in, Skelton had grabbed hold of his leg, and twisted it. He hung on like a leech as the man fell.

Another made the mistake of grabbing Fibula by the scruff of her neck, ready to slam her into the wall. His arm was a bleeding lattice of cuts within seconds.

Another snatched one of Grace's pigtails and dragged her downstairs. Grace banged her mouth on the handrail. Her lip split. He was dragging her back to the kitchen, trying to get her outside. With a violent twist, Grace grabbed the half-brick, and whacked it into the man's elbow. For a few seconds she was free.

Skelton had been punched in the stomach. This hurt. A lot.

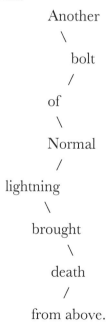

Another
\
bolt
/
of
\
Normal
/
lightning
\
brought
\
death
/
from above.

The man who had been trying to kidnap Grace was now a smoking patch of grease.

At last, the two remaining men retreated, dragging with them the unconscious thug who had been hit by Skelton's cutlass.

They scrambled out from the ruined kitchen doorway, and ran for their lives.

Nobody wanted to follow them.

Grace was on the floor, panting near the oily mess that had been an Ordinary man just a few seconds before. He could have been her dad, Grace thought. If he had been brainwashed into joining the O.P.P. would Yawngrave Tower have killed him too?

Her lip was bleeding. She could hear the others nearby. It was raining so hard now inside the house that those who had clothes found them hanging sodden from their bodies, but the cloud was visibly thinning.

'Thanks to that cloud, I think for now we have won,' said Tibia from the hallway.

Grimsby was wheezing with pain.

'How are you, comrade?'

'Need to get my breath back, that's all,' said Grimsby.

'We've used a few of our nine lives today, my dear,' said Tibia to Fibula, who was limping slightly, her paw bleeding from broken glass.

Skelton leant down and pulled a nasty shard from her paw. Bonaparte too, was picking glass from his knee.

But nobody realised what the battle had really cost them.

Chapter 16

The sorrowful supper

Nobody felt like talking after the fight.

Nobody celebrated.

The mob outside had seen the surviving thugs running for their lives, and their courage wilted, and they melted away in ones and twos. All was quiet on the street, and it was very late. Grace's face was grey with tiredness, but she followed Skelton into the deep puddles and broken glass of his kitchen. It had been devastated. Everything had been torn out of his cupboards and smashed, his ancestral table had been overturned. In the corner the thugs had tried to start yet another a fire but, luckily, the cloud had drenched it before it could do real harm. The back door had been axed and broken open. It now hung at a strange angle, still chained to the locks.

Grace observed the glass in the window frames. The metal bars that protected them had been jemmied and bent, and the remaining glass looked like broken teeth.

She shook her head. Were her eyes that tired? There where blurs in the spaces where there was no glass. The streetlights visible through them seemed to stretch and whorl.

'It's repairing itself,' said Grace, her voice thickened by her swollen mouth.

She wished she had her magnifying glass to examine the weird film of liquid forming in the window frames.

'Look at this!' she said. Skelton leant over to see what she was she had found. As they watched, the glass became more viscous. Until it began to harden into a thicker glass than Grace had ever seen.

Behind them came a tiny *pop-pop pop*. Hundreds of holes were appearing in the floor, as if fish were breaking the still surface of a pond and gulping down the broken glass. After about twenty seconds the little holes were gone, and the floor was smooth. The axe-shattered door creaked and complained, and the split and splintered wood began to cleave and mend, but this time into a substance more like iron than wood. The hinges tightened and straightened. In five minutes Skelton was able to close the door again; in ten minutes it could be locked and bolted.

'Amazing,' said Grace, forgetting the pain in her mouth for a moment. She saw her arm was scratched too. 'It's like scabs. Everything that was hurt has a scab forming on it. Everything is healing and protecting itself.'

'Growing stronger than it was in the first place,' said Skelton.

Next they went into the front room. One of the three sofas was blackened with fire, but Grace noticed that this too was gradually plumping itself back into shape and regaining its golden colour. The rug had been badly scorched but its redness was returning, and the windows were re-growing and the window bars were straightening. The soaked lizard green walls also seemed to have smoothed and repaired themselves. Only the television, which had been kicked to destruction, showed no signs of healing.

Tibia and Bonaparte joined them.

'Shoring up its own defences,' said Tibia admiringly. 'Stronger and stronger.'

'I am beginning to realise,' said Skelton, 'that this house has a mind of its own.'

Grimsby wheezed into the room, and Fibula too.

Rick stayed folded up in the hallway, as if he were asleep.

Flapping agitatedly, Spoony Kooker burst among them. 'I can't find Diana Yellyface.'

Exhausted and hurt as everyone was, they started searching. Guided by Tibia, they worked methodically through the rooms, while Spoony Kooker flitted up and down the Tower calling the moth's full name, 'Diana Anna Indigo Nocturna Tremblina Yellyface...'

Every square inch of the floor and walls and ceiling, had been searched, but the Normal moth was not to be found.

Rick seemed particularly keen to help. Grace wondered if this was because they both could fly, because she could not remember seeing him ever speak to the moth.

Eventually, Fibula said. 'It's no good, Spoony Kooker. It seems she's just not here.'

'Maybe the O.P.P. took her,' wailed the ghoul.

Nobody spoke for a long while.

'We can keep trying,' said Rick.

'You're a good boy,' said Fibula, 'but we must accept that she's—'

'Diana is missing in action,' said Tibia firmly. 'This does not mean she is necessarily...' Tibia paused, and then continued gravely, 'That she is necessarily dead.'

Spoony Kooker refused to give up the search, and tore through the air ever more frantically. With heavy hearts the others eventually climbed up to the War Room, for a much-needed rest.

It was now 3.33 a.m. in the morning of 1 November.

As the others prepared some food, Fibula sat by a window in the War Room. A fire-blackened car had been dumped in Skelton's front garden. It was now being used as an O.P.P observation post. The two men inside it were viewing her with binoculars. She stared back with a twitching tail.

Skelton's fence had been smashed, of course. Half of it had been fed to the flames, and the rest of it turned into orange and purple firewood ready for the next blaze. Behind the ruined car, the bonfires slowly collapsed and smouldered. With her excellent vision, Fibula stared into the shadows beyond the fire, but could see no one.

'We need to eat.' Skelton said.

The Tower yielded secret stores of food. There was a room lined with tins and jars full of all kinds of preserved foods. Many had old-fashioned labels, but when you popped the lids off, the food smelt fresh and appetising.

Skelton helped the cats and Grimsby first, as opening tins is not always easy for them.

The bat boy, meanwhile, quietly selected a jar of locusts, relishing their juicy bodies as he crunched their heads and wingcases.

Around them people were eating what, to Grace, seemed astonishing amounts at once.

'Excuse me, Skelton,' said Grace, 'but I am really hungry. Is there anything here for an Ordinary person?'

'Well, Grace Brown, let me see,' Skelton said, feeling ashamed that the poor girl was hungry in his house. 'I know there are some foods that both Normal people and Ordinary people like. Hmm. Let me see... Do you like eel intestines? Popular with some Ordinary Japanese people?'

'I don't think so,' said Grace.

'Hmm. Lovely crunchy grasshoppers cooked in chilli and garlic are enjoyed in Oaxaca, Mexico by Ordinary people. They're a particular favourite of Bonaparte's. Fancy those?'

Grace pulled a face. 'Not really,' she said.

'Okay,' Skelton said patiently. 'Snake tongues? Rat's ears? Marzipan?'

'Marzipan!' said Grace. 'I love marzipan.'

'Excellent. Marzipan is a very Normal food indeed. And it goes so well with other things. Mmm. Marzipan and mule hoof surprise...' Skelton muttered, drifting off. 'There's a meal with a real kick...'

'Any more?' asked Grace pointedly.

'Frogspawn? Tinned peas?'

'Peas! I can eat peas.'

'Acorns? Jellyfish? Pumpkin puree?'

'Pumpkins!' said Grace.

'Excellent,' Skelton said. 'You have the makings of a nice meal there.

After quickly warming the peas and the pumpkin puree Grace sat at the huge table that had grown out of the floor.

Fibula glanced at her plate. 'I never knew you enjoyed Normal food, my dear,' she said as Grace bit into a big piece of marzipan with a pea stuck to it.

Skelton sat next to Bonaparte, who was playing with a plateful of stewed stinging nettles and rat loins, garnished with wasp-sting sauce. Skelton knew this was one of Bonaparte's top hundred meals, so was concerned that he was eating so slowly.

'What's up, old stick?' he asked quietly.

'To be honest,' said Bonaparte, 'it's that moth. I'm not saying she wasn't annoying – as can quite a few of us can be – but Spoony loves her Skelton and she is missing. Probably dead. To be honest, tonight has been so upsetting that it has almost put me off my food.'

'At least it's quiet outside now,' Skelton said.

Bonaparte shook his head. His face caught the glow from the fires in the street. 'They must be hatching new plots,' he muttered. 'And what about the summons? All it has brought is these two kids, and one of them's Ordinary. And the Normal one's... well, he's strange: he's not to be trusted. When is the real help coming? Perhaps there's only us left. If this is our army against all the evil Mrs Bland can do… what hope do we have?'

Skelton had never seen Bonaparte so worried.

'If we don't fight back, who will?' Skelton said. 'This Tower is full of surprises. It seems to be taking care of us.'

Everyone needed to recover. The two Normal cats already curled up, while Rick wrapped in his own wings with his eyes closed, looked as innocent as a baby. Grace had found a blanket and several pillows and had made a nest for herself. She was also fast asleep.

Even Grimsby's snoring disturbed nobody.

'We're tired now,' Skelton said. 'Things might seem different tomorrow. We'll have to trust the night to protect us.'

There were some sleeping hooks nearby, and they wearily climbed onto them. Resting nicely against the wall, they were soon fast asleep.

As they slept, the house continued to groan and grow and change.

Downstairs, all alone, Spoony Kooker darted around the kitchen and into the hall and the sitting room calling for the Normal moth. His watery heart was full of fear and loss.

Chapter 17

Remote control

'I'm sick of taking orders,' said Rick when the others had left.

After a late breakfast, Tibia had divided his troops into three patrols. They were to return in half an hour with a report of everything they had seen. Skelton, Grimbsy and Tibia had gone to the ground floor, Fibula and Bonaparte to the middle floors, and Grace and Rick were told to climb to the top of the Tower and observe enemy movements.

'Why are you still here?' Rick said to Grace. 'You're not Normal. Why don't you run back to your dear, sweet mother? She's just around the corner.'

'I can't.' Grace blinked fiercely. 'All these O.P.P people – all the Ordinary people, my parents too – have been brainwashed by your stupid mother. It's not fair.'

'Shut up about my mother,' said Rick flaring his wings at her. They stared at each other angrily, until

Rick laughed. 'Not fair?' he said bitterly. 'Not fair! What a child you are.'

'If she's your mother,' Grace said factually, 'she can't be as Ordinary as she says she is.'

'Just shut up. I don't know why I'm speaking to a kid like you.'

'You're a kid too,' said Grace.

'Am I though?' said Rick. He turned his back, and wrapped his wings around him.

'Well, you can do what you want.' Grace said. 'I'm doing what Tibia said, to see if I can make any useful observations from the top.'

Half a dozen spiral staircases now led up from the War Room. Grace right away began climbing the one she remembered from last night. There had been a good view of the street outside.

Today there seemed fewer candles, and Grace wondered if the distances between each candle had increased as Yawngrave Tower spread out in the sky. In the dark, Grace relied on her ears, listening to the scuff of her feet, and the perfectly Normal creaking of each stair as she trod on it.

She ran her finger along the wall as she walked. Its dampness fascinated Grace. It was as if the house was an enormous plant that drew water from its roots to the top of its pointiest turret.

Eventually, from many twists below, came the steady *creak-creak-creak* of someone pacing up the stairs.

'Rick?' she called.

But there was no reply. *Still sulking*, she thought.

'Rick?' she called again.

No reply.

It wasn't the darkness, or the sound of her own breathing, nor even the cramped staircase that made Grace feel nervous. Without thinking, she patted her pocket. Her phone, of course, was long gone.

Soon she had hurried to a tiny arrow's-width loophole, which let in a gasp of fresh air and a sliver of grey daylight from the outside world. She paused here, gratefully.

Below her, the footsteps had changed. Now Rick seemed to be hurrying, bounding two or three steps at a time. Was he flying or gliding? Surely it was too cramped to fly.

'Rick?' she called again.

Nothing.

Grace started to run. She did not know why. It was just a feeling, just something she was imagining. But soon she was running in a blind panic. She had to reach the top of these stairs first.

Rick, if it was Rick, was gaining on her.

'Stop!' Grace shouted. Why was she running? She was being silly, she told herself. It was Rick: he had rescued her, hadn't he? Standing under one of the few candles, she turned to face her fears.

Long seconds stretched out before, bounding up the last few stairs with an angry energy, Rick arrived. His wings were bunched at his shoulders.

The beads of his black eyes gleamed at her, and flickered. His laugh was cold, and it was not his. The laugh was older, smoother and far more evil. His face loomed into the tiny patch of light, but it was different. His mouth lolled open, and his features were a slackened mask.

Mrs Bland's green eyes stared at Grace with icy hatred.

'I might have guessed,' said the voice coming from Rick's mouth.

Grace backed up several stairs, but Rick's puppeted body followed her.

'Well, well. Here we are. Inside Yawngrave Tower,' said the voice.

One of Rick's fists balled, and it thumped on the trickling damp of the Tower's wall. Grace backed up the stairs. And there! At last... was the trapdoor. Grace pushed but the door wouldn't open. There was a heavy latch, and Grace strained at it: one... two...

Bang!

A few inches from Grace's head both of Rick's hands had punched the door with enormous force.

Grace was roughly bundled out onto the platform at the top of the Tower.

It was drizzling, but Grace blinked in the brightness of daylight. She stumbled away from the trapdoor, and noticed one of her knees was bleeding again. Behind her, Rick's body was emerging.

Upright now, his body dangled as if an invisible hand held him by the scruff of his neck. His face was flickering uncertainly, like a candle that guttered in a draught. Sometimes the black eyes were his own, but mostly they blazed with a green fire.

'Rick!' Grace called out in horror.

'Oh don't pity him,' Mrs Bland said.

'You monster. Why don't you leave him alone?' said Grace.

'Oh, I will. Very soon in fact,' said Mrs Bland. 'This little *projection* of mine is tiresome.'

Her eyes surveyed the view. 'I'd forgotten just how beautiful it was,' she said. 'There's the river same as always, and see how many parks there are...' Her voice trailed off. 'He is my flesh, Grace Brown. You can't control him now.'

'Me? I wasn't trying to control him,' said Grace.

'You little witch!' hissed Mrs Bland's voice. 'Just because he has flown away, doesn't mean I can't reach him. Doesn't a mother always have power over her sons?'

'Even the Normal ones?' Grace said.

Mrs Bland's green eyes blazed loathing at Grace. She backed away, till the rampart was solid behind her.

Rick's body leapt up to stand on the rampart. He teetered precariously. The hard ground was far, far below.

'Don't be sad, Grace. Your little Peter Pan has to go now. And by the way. I will tell you something that will stop you from missing him. Have you heard the name – needless to say a *ridiculous* name – Diana Yellyface?'

'Yes,' said Grace.

'Diana Yellyface,' said Mrs Bland, 'was an insect, wasn't she?'

'She is a Normal death's-head hawkmoth,' said Grace.

'And my son thinks he is a bat of some description?'

'Yes...'

'And what do bats like to eat most of all?' Mrs Bland waited. 'Surely someone as *scientific* as you knows the answer to that.'

'Most are insectivores. They eat insects...' answered Grace faintly.

The body teetering on the battlement shuddered. Grace realised Mrs Bland was making it tremble with humourless laughter.

For a second Rick was himself again, staring with astonishment at something just over Grace's shoulder. He gave a strangled cry. Suddenly green-eyed again, his wings folded and his body slowly twisted on the battlement it balanced on.

He dropped.

Grace ran to edge, to peer over the parapet.

The boy was falling like a stone.

'RICK!' she screamed. 'FLY!'

Chapter 18

The shadow under the stairs

Far below Grace, on the ground floor, Skelton, Grimsby and Tibia had checked the locks and chains of the front door, and were now walking into the living room. Overnight its corners had smoothed to gentle curves, so the space seemed less of a box and more of a big bubble in the wood. The scorched rug had regrown like a woolly red lawn, and the sofas were even more squidgy and inviting than before. They dragged the remains of the TV from the room.

Outside, in the street they could see two bored men in grey smoking roll-up cigarettes and glancing at their phones as they sat in the burnt-out car. There was no one else to be seen, and it was beginning to rain.

'I have one question,' whispered Skelton. 'Where are the police? Surely they would have noticed all the O.P.P.'s unspeakable outrages last night?'

'People see what they expect to see,' said Tibia quietly. 'Terrible things happen every day and they are never reported. It seems Mrs Bland could hide her evil in the daylight, in the middle of a busy street and *still* nobody would see it.'

'She certainly makes people feel alone,' said Skelton.

From the kitchen, they peered out into the back garden. The fences were all flattened, and part of the blackthorn hedge had been scorched by fire.

There was nobody to be seen, Normal or Ordinary.

'Perhaps they've given up,' said Skelton.

Tibia shook his head. Neither of them believed it.

Grimsby, who was still new to Skelton's house and full of curiosity, sniffed interestedly at the circular door under the stairs. 'What happened in 1603?' he asked, reading the date carved on it.

'If I remember my lessons from Ye Normal School for Young Gentlefolk,' said Skeleton, 'it was a plague year. About a quarter of the people in London were killed by infected fleas.'

'A dark year,' said Tibia, scratching.

'When did you last open it?' asked Grimsby.

'Ninety-odd years ago,' said Skelton, 'and only for a few seconds. There was nothing in it. Only my pop said there was far too much nothing in it for his liking, and banged it shut again, very quickly.'

'So you saw nothing?' asked Tibia doubtfully.

'Only the second kind of darkness,' said Skelton. 'But there must be an assortment of somethings in it, though, judging by their noises.'

'What sort of somethings?' asked Grimsby. 'Made-up ones like Mr Tumnus the faun from *The Lion The Witch and The Wardrobe*?'

'Of course not,' Skelton said.

'Well, let's have a gander then,' said Grimsby. 'Everything's changing in your home. Maybe there's something useful in it like another armoury or more food. Maybe there are sausages. Maybe there are pies.'

Skelton found *pies* a persuasive thought. After all, what did a few claws scratching on a wooden door, or the occasional perfectly Normal roaring, matter compared to the possibility of discovering a new pie or pasty?

'Right, ho!' he said, much to the others' surprise. Soon he was turning his spider-eyed skeleton key in the lock (with a nicely Normal clunk) then it was just a matter of pulling open the three rusty bolts that had secured the ancient door for hundreds of years.

'Coooeee!' called Grimsby, poking his face into the hole without hesitation. Cold air streamed out of the cupboard, and he half climbed inside. 'It's big,' he said, but his voice sounded deadened, his words like two keys wrapped up in socks and dropped on the floor.

Grimsby pulled his face out again. 'It smells deep,' he said.

'Me now,' said Skelton, elbowing him aside. Tibia poked his head in at the same time. There was nothing to be seen, but something about the atmosphere made them feel they were inside a vast cavern. Skelton sniffed. It was definitely as earthy as Grimsby said, once you had ignored the whiff of sardine heads on Tibia's breath. 'Interesting,' he said. 'I need to explore.'

At that second, pain skewered into both Skelton's thumbs. 'Ouch!' he yelped, bumping his skull as he jerked out of the hole. Tibia's head popped out too. His battered ears were flat against his head and his tail was thick. Grimsby had bared his teeth, and was licking one of his paws.

'Maybe that's not such a good idea,' Skelton said.

'Agreed,' said Grimsby. 'I don't like it. Wild horses couldn't drag me down there.'

'But it has to be said that this is part of Yawngrave Tower,' Skelton said, staring into the black. 'We'll go later. Yes, let's go later when things are more settled. We'll have an expedition!'

'Yes, later,' said Tibia. Even he sounded relieved. 'We've enough trouble in our bowls, without opening the door to more.'

Skelton locked and bolted the circular door.

But it did no good. When he had his back to it, he felt that a dilated black pupil was gazing at him from behind an inch of old wood. As they walked into the front room, he glanced over his shoulder at the round door. *Silly old rattler*, he told himself, *it's just very, very Normal indeed.*

The loud hammering on the front door made Skeleton jump. Beside him, Tibia hissed in alarm.

'Careful!' said Grimsby.

Skelton peered through the spyhole, which was shaped like a carp's head. Both inside and outside was a mouth open in an O of surprise.

The face he saw was upside down. Rick was clinging over the door, his face strangely flushed.

'It's the bat boy,' Skelton said.

'Let him in,' said Grimsby. 'Be quick! He must have flown down from the top. The children may have seen something.'

Skelton hesitated.

'Skelton,' said Grimsby. 'You can't leave the lad out there with the O.P.P.'

Skelton peered out yet again. The two men in the burnt-out car had climbed out. One was filming Rick on his phone. As quickly as possible, Skelton unlocked the door chains and opened the creaking door.

Rick shouldered inside.

'It's not often you bats flap by day,' said Tibia.

'I had to be quick,' said Rick. 'What I saw up there is urgent.'

'Are we under attack again?' asked Tibia.

'No. But it's more important than that. I saw the Golden Cockerel.'

Skelton gaped at him, astonished.

'You saw the...' Skelton began.

'The Golden Cockerel,' said Rick, 'yes.'

'The Golden Cockerel!' Tibia cried, 'I thought that being existed only in legend.'

'It's not. I've seen it,' said Rick, his eyes flashing. 'It is a magnificent bird of golden metal.'

'The bird of omen and truth for all Normal people,' whispered Skelton in awe. 'Here? At Yawngrave Tower? I've never seen it. As far as I know, nobody has seen it for ages.'

'Yes, Skelton. In the upper branches of the Tower. It gave me a message for you.'

'For me?' Skelton said in wonder. Not old Bonaparte, or Tibia, or Fibula, or Grimsby or anyone else, but Skelton Kirkley Elvis Lionel Lupus Yawngrave III had been chosen. 'What did the noble Golden Cockerel have to say to the Master of Yawngrave Tower?' he asked.

'The Golden Cockerel asked me to pass its compliments to the Master of the Tower.' Rick's face twisted strangely here. 'It said this: Yawngrave must go under the stairs. He must explore the dark roots of the world to conquer the besiegers.'

'Are you certain?' Skelton did not like the sound of this.

'Oh yes!' Rick said. 'The Golden Cockerel said this to me personally. It demands that you go under the stairs.'

'I don't know.' Skelton wavered. 'My thumbs...'

'I am just the Golden Cockerel's messenger,' said Rick.

'Don't go, Skelton,' said Grimsby. 'Don't get distracted from the fight we face right here and now.'

Skelton scowled at him. *Even the Golden Cockerel knows I am the Master of this Tower*, he was thinking, *but Grimsby and the rest still think they know better.*

'My thumbs were pricking,' Skelton said, 'but if the Golden Cockerel says I should go there, who am I to disagree?'

'Yes. You must do what the Golden Cockerel says,' said Rick eagerly. 'You must do it now. But there was another instruction. The Golden Cockerel said you shouldn't go alone.'

'Not while there's an army outside—' Tibia began.

'It instructed me to go with you,' Rick interrupted.

'You?' Skelton said, surprised.

'Yes the Golden Cockerel said that we should go together. Down in the roots of the world we will find something to explain...' he paused. 'To explain everything.'

'I don't like the smell of this,' said Grimsby. 'Not one little bit. I say again, don't go Skelly, you'll regret it.'

'Ignore him Skelton, come on!' said Rick.

'Yes,' Skelton said, but he did not move.

'Skelton, a word if I may,' said Tibia. 'I don't think you should go either. It doesn't feel right, and the boy seems in a strange mood.'

'You'd be in a strange mood too if you'd just seen the Golden Cockerel,' Skelton said.

'Listen to Tibia, Skelly,' said Grimsby.

Skelton ignored them, and especially Grimsby (as he ignored anyone who called him *Skelly*).

After taking several seconds unlocking the round door, Skelton, on hands and knees, thrust his head into the damp black hole.

'Skelton, do not go!' Tibia said.

'The fact is, master cat,' said Rick with a sneer, 'that the Golden Cockerel had a message for Skelton because he is your better. Skelton has a vital mission that you wouldn't understand. One that only he can accomplish.'

'That's true enough,' said Skelton, pulling his head back from the dark. 'The bat boy is right. It's my Tower, and the Golden Cockerel chose me to go. Who am I to disagree? And who are you, for that matter. Won't be long!'

Without wasting another moment, Skelton bundled into the damp blackness, quickly followed by Rick. Ahead of them was nothing but the second kind of darkness.

'Skelton, come back you infuriating rattler! Return to your duty,' Tibia called again, but his voice already seemed far away. All around Skelton the darkness was thick and velvety. The only light was a faint circle from the door. Skelton saw the shadows of the jealous heads of Tibia and Grimsby stretching imploringly into the black world. He ignored the last rude cry of *Skelly!* and walked on.

'Good riddance to those losers!' said Rick and laughed with a mirthless clicking that passed between his needle teeth.

His arms stretched out before him, Skelton was comfortable in the dark. This vast space was as quiet as a grave. He guessed it to be an underground cavern, with a gently sloping floor. Once or twice he leant down to touch the ground. It wasn't cold enough to be stone. If anything, it felt like hard wood.

Gradually, as they went deeper, their footsteps found a distant echo, and the air felt less oppressive.

Several times Skelton tried to talk to Rick. The boy would grunt a few syllables in reply. The only sound

Skelton could hear was their own footsteps and, a few paces behind him, Rick's rapid breath.

From time to time Skelton flapped his hands and winced. The pain in his thumbs was for his own good. His thumbs were only trying to warn him.

Chapter 19

The search party

'FLY!' Grace screamed.

The second before he would have hit the ground, Rick's wings snapped open like a black parachute. Grace saw him below, crouched and panting on the garden path. Without looking back at Grace, he quickly scrambled onto the brickwork of the house, to cling upside down, one ear pressed against Skelton's door. She called down to him, but he did not seem to hear her. Eventually she saw Skelton allow him in.

The rain was heavy now. Blood from her cut knee ran thin, dripping onto the slippery platform of the turret. An aircraft poked out from the heavy clouds. Distant cars splashed through puddles.

From just behind her came a whirring sound.

Shocked, Grace span round. There was a huge bird; a cockerel. It advanced towards her, robotically jutting its golden head. Taking a step back, Grace made rapid observations: how each vane on each feather was made of fine filigrees of gold, and how its eyes were like pools of quicksilver.

'Can you speak?' said Grace. The Golden Cockerel adjusted its head, to peer at her with one eye.

'*Yes*,' chimed the bird, taking a step towards her. Grace knew the trapdoor was open. She could run…

'*Stop!*' The word came from somewhere inside its body, like the striking of a grandfather clock.

'Why should I?' said Grace. 'Who are you, and what do you want?'

'*I want you to be angry.*'

'But I hate being angry,' she said. What did it mean?

The metal creature gave no reply. Instead, it appeared to be powering down. It poked its gold-combed head under a golden wing, and became very still.

'*Angry?*' Grace did not think she was feeling angry. She often felt scared, and wanted the O.P.P. and Mrs Bland to go away forever. Was this anger? No. It was more like sadness. She pictured her little sister Molly alone with her brainwashed parents. As tears came to her eyes she reached out to touch the bird, which was as tall as she was. Its metal feathers were impossibly fine and soft, and her fingers sank in a little. She wondered if it was a beautiful robot because it felt so cold to touch.

'Are you asleep?' she asked. The bird did not move.

Suddenly Grace remembered Tibia had sent her and Rick to make observations. There was not time to become distracted, however wondrous this metal being.

Anxiously, Grace saw that a huge truck was crossing the bridge over the muddy river. It was transporting a mechanical digger with a big toothed bucket on its front, used to scoop up rubble and push walls over. The machine seemed freshly painted in grey, and she was sure it was being driven towards them.

Immediately below, the streets were patched with the blackened remains of bonfires. Two grey men were still stationed in the wrecked car but the road was eerily empty. She had seen them observe Rick being let in again... Rick! She must get back to the others to warn them!

But what was this?

Beside her, the Golden Cockerel whirred back into life. It turned its head quizzically towards her.

'Please will you help us?' she asked.

'*You are being helped*,' it fluted, spreading its wings, and launching into the air.

Moments later, Grace was darting between the small islands of candlelight as she descending the twisting stairs.

'At last,' said Bonaparte. He was pacing nervously from loophole to loophole, while trying not to fall into the vault full of spikey weapons in the War Room. Fibula was there too, looking down on the back garden. Skelton, Grimsby and Tibia were downstairs.

'Where's the boy?' asked Fibula, slinking over to the girl.

'He fell off the roof,' said Grace shakily.

'Good thing he possesses wings,' said Bonaparte. He peered at Grace in a concerned way. 'But I can guess, just from your perfectly Ordinary face, that things are bad.'

'It's Mrs Bland...'

'What about her?'

'It's always Mrs Bland,' said Fibula, the claws suddenly hooking out from her six paws, and tapping on the hard floor as she hurried back to her vantage point over the garden.

'She's controlling Rick somehow. Talking through him, making him do things against his will.'

'I *knew* it,' said Fibula.

'And there's another thing... I think Mrs Bland made Rick eat Diana Yellyface.'

'He *ate* her?' Bonaparte said eventually.

'That woman would say anything,' cried Fibula. 'It's too horrible to be true. I won't believe it.'

Grimsby and Tibia had hurried upstairs to join them in the War Room.

'Where's Skelton?' asked Bonaparte.

'He went into the second kind of darkness in the cupboard under the stairs. And Rick's gone with him.' Tibia sighed.

'We thought it was wrong,' said Grimsby. 'The whole idea stabbed our paws.'

'Wrong? *Wrong?*' said Bonaparte heatedly. 'Tell them, Grace!'

'Mrs Bland has taken control of Rick.'

'Eh?' Grimsby said.

'She took over Rick's body. He was like a puppet making weird movements, and she spoke through his mouth.'

'So,' Tibia said slowly, 'I let Skelton enter a paw-prickingly scary hole in the ground, with the bat boy who is controlled by Mrs Bland.'

'But how did this happen?' cried Bonaparte.

'Rick knocked on the front door, and convinced Skelton that the Golden Cockerel had said to go under the stairs,' Tibia continued.

'I saw the golden bird!' said Grace. 'It didn't speak to Rick! It spoke to me after he had fallen.'

'Wait, wait!' said Fibula running across to Grace again. 'You're telling us that you saw the Golden

Cockerel? What did it say to you? An Ordinary girl too...'

'I didn't really understand,' said Grace, 'it said, *I want you to get angry*, and *You are being helped*.'

'Sounds like the sort of thing the Golden Cockerel would say,' said Bonaparte. 'It is supposed to be an enigmatic fowl.'

'Has anyone seen Diana Yellyface?' asked Spoony Kooker for the hundredth time as he melted into the room.

'Spoony my dear,' said Fibula, 'Grace has told us some very bad news.'

The ghoul clenched like a fist in the air.

'Grace says that...' Fibula faltered. 'Grace thinks that Rick may have eaten her.'

'He what?' yelped Grimsby, in horror.

Spoony said nothing. For a few seconds he was like a fiery red flag snapping in the wind. Then he was gone.

There was a rumble in the street outside.

Fibula sprang to the window. A grey excavator was pulverising what remained of Skelton's little fence, crushing it under its caterpillar tracks like matchsticks.

'The digger!' said Grace. 'I meant to say.'

Rushing to the loopholes, now everyone could see with their own eyes.

'We'll need more than goo to repel that,' said Tibia gravely. He knew better than anyone: their weapons were inadequate. What use was a dusty collection of antiques, useless suits of armour, and long pikestaffs that none of them except Bonaparte and Skelton could even hold?

The great machine was powering straight for the foot of Yawngrave Tower. It had a massive steel toothed bucket at the end of a long jointed arm. Fibula hissed. Her back arched.

BOOM!

A shudder went through the whole Tower. It almost knocked Grace and Bonaparte from their feet.

'It bounced off!' said Fibula amazed. Her thirty claws had kept her hooked to the windowsill. 'The Tower is strong!'

'Grimsby, Bonaparte, come on. Let's pour some goo on it,' said Tibia, heartened a little. 'At the very least it will make it slippery work for them.'

But Bonaparte didn't move. 'What about Skelton?' he said. 'Skelton's gone into a dark hole with that dratted bat boy. We can't leave him to be ambushed all alone in the second kind of darkness.'

'There's fighting to be done here,' said Tibia sternly.

'He's right,' said Grimsby.

'But I *have* to find the old buffoon,' said Bonaparte. He was torn. 'That antique numbskull is my best friend and I can't just let him walk into a trap. Besides he might have found an escape route, if the Tower falls. There are loads of tunnels under London.'

'I agree,' said Grace unexpectedly. 'It's not Rick's fault; he can't help it when Mrs Bland controls him. I'll come with you.'

'You will?' said Bonaparte in relief. For he dreaded the thought of the hole, for unlike most Normal people Bonaparte was extremely scared of the dark. 'Let's get them.'

BOOM! Candles dropped from their holders, and ancient dust was disturbed throughout the Tower.

'Okay,' said Tibia irritably. 'Try to find Skelton if you must. But it's a poor strategy to desert your posts when you're under attack.'

He turned his attention to the others.

'Grimsby, Fibula my dear,' he said gravely, 'we three must stand alone to protect Yawngrave Tower at all costs. This is the last outpost of Normal decency and it has to be saved. Those people out there are dangerous. We must remember that they are still people. Just very silly ones that are easily led. We must do whatever we can to keep them out. This may be our last battle. With luck they won't win it in minutes.'

Fibula rubbed her face against Tibia's battered old head, but said nothing.

'All I can say,' growled Grimsby, 'is that I hope that old coffin dodger is grateful, wherever he is.'

'Good luck Bonaparte, good luck Grace,' said Tibia.

For once Bonaparte was stuck for something to say, until he blurted out, 'Good luck to you too. And sorry for being a deserter and for calling you weasels all those times.'

'Well, Boney,' began Fibula, 'we're sorry for calling you—'

A sound like a cracking whip made everyone jump.

It was Spoony Kooker. But a Spoony who was changed utterly. The ghoul had become fierce and flame-like. His edges were harder, and he emitted a harsh cry that flattened even Tibia's battered old ears.

'I am going to frighten them,' said Spoony Kooker. Before anyone could speak, he passed through the Tower wall easily as light through glass.

They heard his hair-raising howl as he arrowed down. In answer, there was a desperate wail from the O.P.P. driver, suddenly trapped in his cabin with an appalling apparition.

'Blooming marvellous!' cried Grimsby, amazed. 'He's terrifying!'

The Ordinary man in the digger began whimpering like a child. He scrambled from his driver's cab and ran towards the end of the street, hotly pursued by a howling red ghoul, and even the two men in the burnt-out car dropped their binoculars and ran for their lives.

'Go now,' said Tibia, turning to Grace and Bonaparte, 'this is a good moment. But hurry!'

'Get cracking!' said Fibula.

Bonaparte and Grace rushed down the musically creaking stairs to the hallway of the ground floor. From outside came faint, bloodcurdling shrieks. Whatever Spoony was doing to the men out there, it was still working.

Grace had courageously controlled her feelings about the dark in Charcoal House. The darkness under the stairs felt much worse. She could not bring herself to step into this black hole and the fact that Bonaparte's teeth were chattering did not help her.

Abruptly, however, he spidered one of his long legs into the dark.

'Stop, Bonaparte! Did Skelton have a torch?' *Why*, Grace thought, *don't Normal people ever seem to think about things like torches?*

'No he likes darkness, a lot more than I do. He doesn't have much time for torches...' He glanced at Grace. 'You don't have to roll your eyes like that.'

Bonaparte withdrew his foot from the black hole, and thought for a moment. 'Ah-ha! He does have a bicycle, an old penny farthing.' He grinned at her, 'I have always wanted his bicycle, but he has refused to give it to me. I think it has lights on it.'

He led them to a storage area near the kitchen, full of rusty pots and pans, and discarded pie paraphernalia, such as pie chimneys, pie dishes, pie tins, pie slicers and so on.

Under a canvas cover was a stately old bicycle. Its front wheel was tall as Grace, while its rear wheel was tiny. There was an impressive brass horn too, shaped like a trumpeting elephant. But there were two very modern bicycle lights on it – a red one and a white one. With some fiddling they freed them from their housings.

They returned to the circular doorway.

'Ow-ow!' said Bonaparte, almost dropping one of the bicycle lamps to shake his thumbs. 'To be perfectly honest with you, Grace Brown,' he said, 'I am a bit nervous about this even with a torch. You don't have to come with me. There's no point in two of us having to be terrified.'

'I'm scared too, Mr Bonaparte, but if we go together we will be a bit less frightened than if one of us went on our own.'

'You are a remarkable whippersnapper,' said Bonaparte, secretly relieved. 'Let's go before you change your mind.' He bravely poked his head into the black, and his body followed. Grace took a deep breath and pulled herself through the circular hole after him.

They stood inside the entrance. Before them was the opposite of sunshine, the opposite of the moon and stars, the opposite of lightbulbs and screens and sparks and fires and windows. It was the second kind of darkness, and in it they could see nothing.

Bonaparte did not move.

'Mrs Bland said Normal people liked the dark,' said Grace.

'Don't say her name!' said Bonaparte sharply. 'Not here.'

'Sorry,' said Grace.

'But she's right. Most Normal people do,' said Bonaparte more kindly. 'But everyone is different. The second kind of darkness has' – *clack* – 'always scared me.'

'My dad used to say that being brave means doing things that frighten you,' said Grace. 'But that was before he changed...'

Bonaparte smiled down at the remarkable girl. 'You're a brave person Grace. Come on. Let's both be courageous. We have lamps!'

Grace switched on the bicycle light. The frail beam illuminated nothing more than motes of dust, and a patch of featureless dark floor. She directed it towards Bonaparte. He was shaking his shiny white head.

'Skelton really is *the* most' – *clack* – 'annoying person in the entire world,' he said.

Chapter 20

Wormhole

For half an hour Skelton and Rick had been walking along the bottom of an immense tunnel. It delved so deeply into the earth, they had not heard the grey digger's attack on Yawngrave Tower.

The bat boy made a click with his mouth.

'What are you doing?' asked Skelton.

'Echoes,' sneered Rick. 'One of my *special* powers.'

'No need for that tone,' Skelton said. 'I can't hear anything.'

'No, it's too high-pitched,' said Rick. 'Your ears are a joke.'

'A joke?' Skelton said. 'There's nothing wrong with my ears. Having fine, diminutive ears is a noble trait of the Yawngrave line.' It was so quiet, Skelton could hear Rick's face stretching. He was no doubt mocking him in the dark.

'And what do your echoes say?' he asked him.

'We are in a big tunnel.'

They walked on. Skelton was not fond of silence. 'What did the Golden Cockerel say about me?'

'Not again,' said Rick. 'The bird said that you should *explore the dark roots of the world to conquer the besiegers* or whatever.'

'The *bird*,' Skelton said indignantly. 'Show respect. Meeting the Golden Cockerel was a great honour. He only appears when there's a storm brewing. Even Ordinary people used to understand that, with sensible weathercocks on old houses, towers and steeples.'

'Whatever,' said Rick, sounding bored. He clicked again. 'There's something ahead, a wall I think.'

Skelton put out his arms, and soon he was touching a cold surface, covered with large diamond-shaped tiles. If it was a wall, it had an unusual shape. It bowed out in the middle, and curved away at the top and bottom. As far as he could tell, it was about two metres in height, and was like a giant cylinder lying on its side.

He leant against it for a moment.

'To think all this is part of Yawngrave Tower. Who would have thought it? But what else is down here, other than this,' he kicked his heel at the object he leant against, 'and a bazillion bucketsful of the second type of darkness. What do your echoes tell you, Rick?'

'That I have good ears, Yawngrave,' said Rick irritably.

Skelton didn't say anything for a while. He had noticed that Rick had stopped being annoying. He was now being *extremely* annoying.

'I will remind you that you are still a guest at Yawngrave Tower,' Skelton said, 'and I would like you to show me more respect.'

'What makes you think,' said Rick, 'that this belongs to you?'

'Because we reached it from underneath my stairs,' said Skelton.

'You're so vain.' Rick snickered nastily again. 'You might as well say that London belongs to you because you can reach it from your front door.'

Skelton had no answer to this. Irritably, he reached into his pockets for eatables. All he could find was a handful of cactus spines, which he crunched.

Rick was still laughing at him.

'Will you stop it!' Skelton said. The boy was infuriating.

'I am laughing at your absurd arrogance.' There was something wrong. Rick's voice sounded different.

Skelton felt as if he had woken from a disturbing dream only to find that being awake was worse. 'What am I doing here?' he whispered to himself.

The thoughts that slunk next into his brain, gave him no comfort. First, he had only Rick's word that he had seen the Golden Cockerel, or the bird as he insultingly called it. Second, did he trust Rick? The boy had plainly tricked him by appealing to the pride of the Yawngraves. A nasty idea. Third, what on earth was he doing down here in the dark, when his house was being attacked? And, fourth, why was it so important for Rick to get him alone in the dark, hours from anyone that could help him?

'I'm going home right now.' Skelton said abruptly. 'My house is at the mercy of your mother's grey thugs, and yet I am here chasing wild geese with a bat boy.' He pictured Bonaparte, Fibula and Tibia and the others desperately fighting for the safety of Yawngrave Tower. A wail of remorse escaped his mouth. He had been a vain, silly bonehead.

He turned on his heels on the damp, uncertain floor. 'My friends need me. I'm off,' he said.

'I don't think so.'

Skelton froze. Not because this was an annoying thing to say (which of course it was) but because of who said it. There are some voices you know instantly, even deep underground.

'Skelton Yawngrave. It has been a long time.'

'How...?' Skelton felt a cold splash trickle down his spine.

'It's typical to find you stumbling around in the dark,' continued the voice. 'You're clueless aren't you?

Round and round, round and round. Till you all fall down.'

'You!' Skelton whispered. 'How have you done this?'

'He is mine, isn't he? If I cannot control my own sons, what example would I be setting to the world?'

A groan escaped from Rick's body. Rick was there too, somewhere, crushed under the weight of his mother's hateful presence.

The voice, however, was coaxing, almost warm. 'Skelton why do you oppose me? It is not just me who thinks it is time for change. Everyone does. Think about it: Normal people like you are so few these days, clinging to your traditions, breaking the rules of Ordinary behaviour. You are ugly fossils, from a time gone by,' she said, but her voice was still honey-sweet. 'It is important Skelton, to face the truth. You live in a dream world. What is it this week? Recipes?' she laughed scornfully. 'Dressing up in gaudy clothes? Facts are facts, Skelton. Normal People should be in circuses or jails. Soon there will be a time when Normal people will just be memory, a fairy tale to make Ordinary children laugh. Be realistic Skelton,' she purred.

Of course she was right, Skelton thought. He was being a fool. Nobody could fight Mrs Bland's changes...

You must resist!
Resist her!

Yes resist!

Women's voices! The same ones Skelton had heard kneeling by his dead father. He snapped free of his dejected thoughts.

'Madam,' Skelton stammered, 'do you think that I want to be a legend or a fairy tale character? I have every bit as much right to live as you have. And besides, I know all about you...' he said.

'You do?' said Mrs Bland, dangerously.

'If you are so Ordinary,' Skeleton said, 'how is it that your son is Normal? Either his father was Normal. Or you are...'

There was a gasp in the dark. He could hear Rick's body being shaken in anger.

'Yes, that's it, isn't it?' said Skelton. 'You are Normal. Who are you really?'

But something was happening. With a rasp, Rick's wings had curved around Skelton in the dark.

'I am the Queen of Shadows,' she hissed. 'I am not Normal or Ordinary. I belong to no one. And I am everywhere!'

Desperately Skelton slid away, back pressed to the wall, which gave a distinct tremble.

Was this a tremor in the earth's crust? Or was something terrible happening to Yawngrave Tower far away, on the surface?

Skelton cried out at the thought.

Mrs Bland laughed harshly. 'Screaming? Skelton, you death's head! You dunce! You child!'

'I am one hundred and...' Skelton began. 'Ouch!'

The boy's wing had struck him, and he fell back, in an indignant rage. '*The rudeness!*' he shouted. Knuckly bits of a wing smashed his head. It hurt. He staggered against the barrier, which again seemed to shift by the merest millimetre or two.

'Why do you hate me?' he cowered blindly, waiting for the next blow.

'Because you are the worst of the Normals.'

Another whistling whack slammed into Skelton's shoulder. Mrs Bland was using Rick's echo detection sense to find him.

A rasping of something enormously heavy.

Cling to it. Come to us!

The wall... No the *thing* was definitely in motion. Skelton turned swiftly and leapt blindly, scrambling to the flatter bit on top. Here he slid about for a moment, yelping in alarm. With no time to think, he clamped his arms and knees, and with his long fingers, dug into the spaces between the big diamond-shaped tiles.

Another whoosh in the air. This time he ducked, just managing to dodge the crunch from Rick's wing.

'Ever played snakes and ladders, Skelton?' said the voice behind him, followed by a fit of Mrs Bland's laughter.

'Where am I going?' Skelton wailed. Whatever it was, was definitely moving. No! The word was *slithering*. It was alive. He was astride a great body.

Down to the roots of the world.

It has been woven.

The voices again. Instinctively, he trusted them. Grace Brown would not have approved. It was not scientific, but compared to Mrs Bland's crazed laugh, which was now disappearing behind him, the voices felt good and safe.

The enormous body was picking up speed. Skelton closed his eyes, his fingers clawing a bony grip in the creature's scales. For now he realised he was on a serpent the size of a London Tube train. But instead of being snug inside a carriage, he was on the roof, clinging on for dear life, something (as any Londoner could tell you) that is one of the stupidest things you could ever do.

There was a glimmer of light ahead. If Skelton had wanted a better view of the dragon-headed monster he rode on, he now had it. Above his head, were a million woven roots, some of them as thick as tree trunks. As he sped on he glimpsed small birds with beady eyes. The closer the serpent drew to the light, the narrower the tunnel became.

They were hurtling so fast that when a straggly root whipped by him, it tore the shoulder of his jacket. He pressed as hard as he could into the diamond scales of the enormous snake.

Blinding sunlight.

And falling! The tunnel had ended, and the snake was careering through thin air, violently whipping its gigantic body.

Wailing, Skelton lost his grip. He was flung into the blue.

Nearby was a beautiful wooded island. Just before he hit seawater with a resounding smack, Skelton saw the sea boiling as the serpent coiled into the deep.

He saw no more.

Chapter 21

No!

Flung from the back of a great serpent, and sinking like a lead weight in water, Skelton reflected that he had always enjoyed swimming pools. He liked doing lengths along the bottom, and craning his neck to watch swimmers splashing on the surface.

Usually, his visits to the pool were uneventful. Once in a while, however, they were very eventful indeed. This usually started with someone pointing and dancing about in agitation. Others would grab long hooks and poke them down into the water at him. At this point a lifeguard would dive in, shout with bubbles, and drag him to the surface.

On such occasions, Skelton would explain that it is perfectly Normal to be scrambling along on the bottom of the pool. Despite this, however, people would get cross and tell him this is a *swimming* pool not a *crawling about on the bottom* pool.

When Skelton responded to these people with the argument that he had negative buoyancy and didn't have a lot of blubber to keep him afloat like some people obviously did, this did not always calm things down. In fact, on at least two occasions, Skelton had been asked to leave. This, of course, was unfair.

So when he found he was lying dazed on the seabed with a prawn picking at the bridge of his small nose, he did not panic. The water was very clear, and the seabed shelved steeply up to the island he had glimpsed in mid-air.

He righted himself and, carefully avoiding an evil-faced conger eel grinning at him from a gap in the rocks, he began to scramble over the seabed towards the shore. Soon the water grew shallower, and warmer. He nibbled experimentally on one or two stinging anemone tentacles and a ragworm, before his head broke the surface. He gratefully gasped lungfuls of fresh air.

He waded through the breaking waves onto the beach, which was surrounded by high granite cliffs. Although there was nobody to be seen, he stood behind a large rock, as he took off his sodden clothes and wrung the salty water from them.

Amazingly, Skelton's shoes had remained on his feet. Standing with sand between his toes, he sloshed seawater from them and wrung his socks out too. He spread his footwear on a rock to dry.

Hanging over the sea was something Skelton had never seen. A circle of darkness, like a black moon in the blue sky. Perhaps, he thought, this was the end of the snake's hole he had fallen from.

The sun and sky puzzled him. How could a *sea* hidden under London?

The rocky beach appeared real enough. Th was squiggled with worm casts, and gobies and flitted in rock pools. He tapped a limpet from the and held it between his fingers.

'Is this island underneath my house in Londoi are we somewhere else?' he asked.

The limpet said nothing, so Skelton ate it. He not sure if Normal limpets existed, but he was p' he had checked.

Skelton followed his feet. Re-socked and shoed, appeared to want to climb up the single path tha up from the beach. The walk uphill was hot work, anc the strong sun made his clothes steam.

The path led into a green valley, from which rose, high and solitary, a thickly wooded hill. A calm, daydreamy mood had settled on him as he walked, so when a woman's voice in his head said:

Climb to us.

He obeyed. He had forgotten all about the siege of his home.

That was until he found he had reached the foot of the hill. His throat was still parched from salt, so as soon as he saw a stream, he fell to his knees to scoop fresh water into his mouth. The water gurgled raucously, almost as if it were talking to him...

'Skelly! Skelly!
You're all bones,
And your Daddy's smelly...'

The song glooped from a watery mouth under a stone, and insulting laughter welled up from several other places. There *were* voices! Not like the special voices in his head. These were different, as if the people who had made him feel freakish and horrible had found a watery mouth.

You stinking skeleton!
You Normal freakshow!
Oi! Bone brain!
Fracture face!
Skeleton!
Skelly!
Skullface!'

Skelton tried to tear himself away from the spiteful water. He staggered one or two steps uphill.

'*You won't go up there,*' said a sneering voice. '*You're all talk, Yawngrave. A coward with no backbone, which is* ironic.'

It was Norbert from *Ye Normal School for Young Gentlefolk*. A bully who had punched Skelton every single day they were at school together.

'*No of course you can't come to my party*,' said a girl called Yasmina, '*Look at your face. You realise that you're not like the others, don't you? You shouldn't be seen in public, let alone come to my house. Ugly!*'

'*There should be places for freaks like you, you old skeleton!*' It was the gruff Ordinary man who had shouted at Skelton only last week. All he had done was tap his silver-topped cane on the floor and hum innocently to himself.

'*Why don't you keep quiet?*' the man said scornfully. '*You're not funny, you're disgusting.*'

The voices, both Normal and Ordinary, were swelling in a crescendo of *rudeness*.

Finally a single voice rose above all of them, sinister and magnetic.

'*Skelton Kirkley Elvis Lionel Lupus Yawngrave III*,' a water-mouthed Mrs Bland said. When she spoke, Skelton felt his name sounded completely ridiculous. He felt ashamed of everything it stood for.

Just water over the stones.

This voice was different. It was kind.

'That's right. It's just water,' Skelton said, 'and I've had enough.'

207

Suddenly he was very fed up. He was hungry. He wanted to listen to the tut of his old clock at home in the Long Room. He wanted to know that Bonaparte was going to call around in half an hour to show off his new cufflinks. Surely that wasn't too much to ask?

'*Ugh*,' said the water. But it was in the voice of a red-faced man wearing huge boots who had shouted at Skelton in the street. '*It shouldn't be allowed! You've no right to be on the streets, going around frightening children.*'

'I have as much right as you do! No!' Skelton shouted. 'No! No! You horrible people!' He shouted down the voices, and stamped up the hill, drawn there by a force that was far bigger than Skelton Yawngrave or the hateful water.

Every time he put his foot down, he shouted aloud.

'NO!' to people who had put him down.

'NO!' to people who made him feel different.

'NO!' to people who hated him for no reason.

In this way Skelton stamped up an ancient stone pathway running next to the brook. Branches wove together overhead, and the path was hedged-in with banks of earth and granite so that it appeared to be a passage with a roof of leaves.

'NO! NO! NO!'

Shouting made him feel strong and proud. Eventually, as the hurtful voices faded and failed Skelton gave his throat a well-earned rest. It was still hot, and the sun wormed through the branches onto his shiny head.

He decided to cool his feet in the stream. Now his shoes had dried, they had become sweaty and hot.

'*Ugh-ugh-ugh*,' said the stream, as he plunged in his aromatic toes.

'Serves you right,' he said.

Chapter 22

Three sisters

Wake up Skelton.

With a start, Skelton pulled his feet out of the argumentative water. He knew the voice. It was different from the others, and hearing it gave him a cold thrill.

Having slipped his shoes back on, he took a decisive step towards the shadows ahead.

The air did something weird, humming and vibrating around him. His skin prickled.

Join us.

He took another step. A shocking spark snapped from one of his fingers. He yelped in surprise.

Everything had stopped. No bird cheeped. No leaf rustled in the wind. In fact, there was no breeze at all. He reached up and touched the open wing of a sparrow suspended in mid-air above his head.

Unlike the bird, he could still move, and so could the three women he now saw sitting below a spreading yew tree. He gaped at them in astonishment. They appeared to be sisters, whose unfathomably dark eyes were all now turned on him.

One of them beckoned him to approach, and Skelton felt curiously bashful as he stepped closer.

The sisters were working on a vast embroidery. Their long, dextrous fingers held needles and strands of vibrantly coloured thread, and the sewn cloth shimmered. It depicted distant lands, icy poles, deserts with purple skies, and choppy seas troubled by marine monsters. Skelton saw the sun and moon, every known planet, and constellations of stars all visible at the same time in a dark blue sky. As he peered closer, a host of faces gleamed up like sequins from the mazy patterns of city streets.

Despite the beauty of this cloth, Skelton's attention was drawn magnetically to the women. He cleared his throat.

'Hello ladies. I am Skelton Kirkley Elvis Lionel Lupus Yawngrave III,' he said, bowing awkwardly.

'My name is Skuld, I am known as the Mother of Being' said one of the women, glancing up from her work, her fingers still busy. She had a strong face that made Skelton feel strong too, just by being near her. Her voice was rich and dark. Then, with a thrill of recognition, he knew this was one of the voices he had heard in his head. 'It is good to see the person you are becoming, Skelton,' Skuld continued, 'for we wove the life into you; we wove your very bones.'

The person I am becoming? thought Skelton.

'Skelton, My name is Verthani, the Mother of Necessity.' This sister's eyes were compelling, and full of the second kind of darkness. 'I am the reason you began your journey. I wove Rick Bland, and the Golden Cockerel and Grace Brown into your pattern. I drew you through darkness to be here. Do you know why?'

'No, not really,' stammered Skelton.

'Skelton.' The third voice flashed like a scarlet leaf in a green wood. Its sound was both sweet and painful. 'You were fated to come here. I am Urth and I am the Mother who is the Weaver of Fate. I wove this return into your story at the time of your birth.'

'Are you saying,' Skelton said, 'I had no choice but to come here?'

'Yes, your thread was woven and this was the time,' said Urth simply.

'But,' Skelton said, 'what about me? Surely I had something to do with it. What about the things I decide for myself? Are you saying that if I'm hungry for a pie on a Tuesday morning, that this is something that was foretold for me? I don't understand.'

The sisters laughed.

'Understanding will come,' said Skuld.

'The first step of your wisdom is taken here,' said Urth.

'But there is still a very long journey ahead,' said Verthani, and the three sisters laughed again. They were mocking him, but in a strangely loving way.

'Skelton,' said Skuld, 'where is your mother?'

The question shook Skelton. Embarrassed and confused, he clamped his jaws shut.

'Did you never think it was strange that you have no mother?' asked Skuld in her dark voice.

Still he said nothing.

'How do you think you came into being?' asked Verthani.

'I don't know,' Skelton said heavily. 'My father never mentioned it. I knew it was something we should never speak about.'

'Indeed,' said Urth, glancing at her sisters. 'We will speak about it now, Skelton. This may surprise you. But we are your mothers.'

'How can I have three mothers?' Skelton wailed.

'Skelton Yawngrave. You are not made like other people. You are different even to Bonaparte.'

Verthani, stood up. Much to Skelton's confusion, she took his hand. 'We built you Skelton, from bones of the dead. We wove sinews, wove muscles and skin, wove your heart and your mind. We wove life itself back into you. But most importantly, we wove our love into you.'

Confused, Skelton gulped. Verthani did not release his hand.

'With your life comes responsibility. You are twice born. You carry the hopes of ancestors, and the hopes of the unborn. This is your time Skelton, when you prove the value of the life you have been given.'

'Wait!' Skelton said. It was too much to take in. 'You're saying I am different from other people?'

'Yes. You are different,' said Skuld. 'Fate, Being and Necessity are your mothers. And now this time is your time to grow up.'

'But,' Skelton said, 'I am grown up. I am one hundred and—'

'Everyone must continue to weave their story,' said Skuld. 'When they stop they will die.'

'Die,' echoed Urth and Verthani.

'But... But I don't want to be part of anything important,' said Skelton. 'I am not a brave person. I'm not a clever person. I'm scared of so many things. In fact you are scaring me really badly right now.'

'You are yourself. We hope it may be enough. The fight has started, Skelton. You are already resisting Ann Bland, as it was foretold. The time for fear is past.'

Skelton shuddered at hearing them say Mrs Bland's name. It belonged far away, to London and on the lips of street thugs. It stood for a cold spirit who could use her own son like a puppet.

'But how can I change who I am? You're telling me to fight her. How am I supposed to do that? Yawngrave Tower is under attack, and I have only a few friends. How can we fight against millions of Ordinary people who have been tricked into believing in a madwoman?'

'With three weapons, Skelton,' said Verthani. 'First you have your friends. And you must count Grace as one of these.'

Skelton nodded. He liked the child, even though he would prefer it if she stopped rolling her eyes all the time.

'You have your courage,' said Skuld.

'Me?' Skelton said. 'Courage?'

'And finally you have your destiny,' said Urth. 'Know this Skelton: Ann Bland is woven into your story. Of all the people in the world she fears you the most.'

'Me?' Skelton laughed so hard it was almost rude. 'Why would she worry about *me*?'

'Concentrate, Skelton!' said Urth. 'You must remember what we are telling you now. It is time to weave yourself into the world. Do not hide: fight. Do not give in: resist. Believe you can change the world for good. Will you do this?'

'I will try my very best,' Skelton said.

'And you are right,' Urth continued with a gentle laugh. 'The pattern of your life is woven by us, but we do not make your decisions about when to eat a pie. What happens now is up to you. All we can say for sure is that at this moment, your colourful thread is prominent in the world, my dear.'

Skuld and Urth stood up, and joined Verthani. Each laid a hand on Skelton.

'But know this, Skelton. We are proud of you, and we believe in you. And right here, right now, we surround you with our protection. We love you. You are our son.'

Skelton suddenly felt like crying. Making tears was difficult for him, but three drops squeezed from his left eye. Other than Pop Yawngrave, nobody had ever said they loved him. Nobody had ever said they believed in him.

'Here,' said Verthani, taking a brooch from her cloak. 'It will remind you of us, and it will bring you luck when you most need it.'

The brooch she put into Skelton's hand was a triangle made of a woven pattern of gold. It was very handsome; it gleamed in Skelton's palm. At its heart was a triangular space.

Skelton stared at it. How could he have forgotten? He fished about in his jacket pocket, with a feeling of dread. Had he lost it in the sea? There! Skelton thanked his Normal stars, for he had found the pin his father had given him, still fastened inside his jacket pocket where he had kept it for safety.

'Does it fit?' asked Verthani.

Skelton slid the tiny triangular pin into the heart of the brooch. They were made for each other. He felt as if he were uniting his mothers with old Pop Yawngrave. It made a beautiful whole.

'A triangle within a triangle: the Pin of Knots,' said Skuld. We are woven together Skelton. Remember this. Part of the person you are is other people. Other people will help you.'

Skelton stammered out a 'thank you', but it seemed inadequate. The Pin of Knots was beautiful, of course. But being with his mothers made him feel as if everything inside him was rearranging itself. He felt he was glowing with warmth, and braver than he had ever been in his life. It is no small thing to meet your mother for the first time. To discover you have three of them, and that they all wanted the best for you, was a lot to understand.

'Goodbye Skelton. Remember, you are not alone. You carry our love with you,' said Skuld.

Her dark voice was becoming faint; the sisters were fading in broad daylight. They grew fainter. Fainter still.

They were gone.

Skelton had been grinning happily at his mothers but now his smile left him. He felt horribly alone, trapped in a bubble of frozen time like an ant in amber. He reached up to touch the sparrow suspended in mid-air. As he did so, the air rippled, and the bird swooped away, and the stream rushed merrily. *They said I carry their love with me*, he thought.

It rained suddenly and very hard. Water streamed over Skelton's face as he turned it towards the sky. It felt good. With no real plan other than that of returning to the beach, he stumbled downhill. Beside him, the stream had nothing to say.

'Three mothers,' he said aloud. He felt fabulous. He began to pity the Normal or Ordinary people who rub along with just one or two mothers. 'Three!' he said aloud again, picturing himself at home, explaining to his friends that not only did he have three mothers, but that they were queenly and magical women who were proud of him.

By the time Skelton had reached the beach, the rain was long gone. It was nearing sundown. There was no sign of the serpent, but the hole in the sky remained. How would he ever be able to reach it?

Exhaustedly he chose a tree above the water line, and found a couple of branches, which made quite satisfactory bed hooks.

Just as he was growing comfortable, a large fierce-eyed seagull landed on his arm, with a very Normal glint in its yellow eyes. Very soon a flock had gathered around him. Dozens of birds: gulls and the beady-eyed darklings he had glimpsed in the tunnel, were settling on his shoulders and pecking at his trousers.

'What do you want?' Skelton asked nervously.

'You,' said the gull.

Chapter 23

A dark discovery

They had been in the darkness under the stairs several minutes before Bonaparte's teeth had stopped chattering. Grace had not been able to think of anything to say as they followed the beam of the bicycle lamp, which cast a tiny ellipse of light on the floor. Grace wished she had her magnifying glass with her to make detailed observations. She had a theory that the ground they walked on was a kind of hard wood. The same wood that formed the new turrets of Yawngrave Tower, whose branches were somewhere far above them in west London. From shining the lamp in all directions, Grace decided they were in an immense hollow root.

'Do you think we are still somewhere under London?' asked Grace.

'Don't!' said Bonaparte. 'Thinking about it makes it worse. Somewhere under hundreds and hundreds and hundreds of crushing tonnes of clay and wormy earth. Waiting to be buried alive—'

'Okay thanks!' interrupted Grace quickly. A big drop of water fell out of the dark and pinged the top of her head. She pointed the lamp upwards. High above them on the curved ebony ceiling, were a dozen dripping stalactites. If this was a hollow root, it must have been here long enough for stalactites to form. She could see no stalagmites on the ground. Perhaps, she thought, something had crushed them before they could grow.

'I don't know *exactly* where we are,' said Bonaparte, more steadily this time. His face even paler than usual when the torchlight caught him. 'In theory we should just be a few minutes' walk from under the stairs. But Yawngrave Tower is full of surprises, and not all of them are nice ones. There's only one way to see how far we've come,' he said grimly. 'Turn off the lamp.'

Surprised, Grace did as she was told.

'Let's wait for our eyes to adjust,' he said in a wavering voice. 'Now Grace, can you see the cupboard door we climbed through? We did leave it—' *clack* '—open, didn't we?'

They both peered backwards into the black, and sure enough there was the tiniest pinprick of grey light. It seemed they hadn't walked in a straight line either, as the grey speck was high above them, to their right.

Grace heard another smothered *clack* or two from Bonaparte's teeth.

'A sinister course, descending slowly, and a long way from safety,' Bonaparte muttered, before quickly adding, 'Please turn the lamp on again now.'

Grace heard him sigh with relief as the patch of floor appeared again.

'We should keep going,' Bonaparte said heavily. 'Skelton needs to be warned about Rick.'

'Okay,' said Grace, but thinking about Rick meant it was her turn to be nervous.

'Come on, Grace Brown,' said Bonaparte. 'We'll be okay if we stick together.'

They moved on.

Neither of them wanted to be the first to mention that their lamplight was becoming weaker and more yellow. Eventually there was no hiding it.

Bonaparte tested the red lamp he had been carrying. To their relief the red glow was strong, but he turned it off.

'There's nothing to see here, Grace Brown. We may as well rely on our ears. Why don't you switch your torch off too for a bit? We might need both of them later.'

It was one of the bravest things that Bonaparte had ever said.

With a sinking feeling, Grace turned off her lamp. She reached out and took Bonaparte's thin hand in her own. Like two blind cave creatures, they walked on, delving ever deeper.

'Skelton!' Bonaparte called for the hundredth time.

'Skelton!' cried Grace too, her voice forlorn in the brooding dark.

'Grace,' said Bonaparte, sniffing. 'I think I can smell something. Can you?'

Grace sniffed. 'The air seems fresher,' she said. 'There's a bit of a breeze here.'

'If this tunnel is taking us towards fresh air, it makes sense to follow.'

They walked on further. The ground began now to slope downwards ever more steeply. Occasionally Bonaparte turned on his red lamp to make sure of their footing.

After a while he spoke again, 'I'm very worried about that old creaker. I don't want him to – you know – die or anything.'

They walked on in silence, and Grace heard him gulping in the dark. She kicked something hard on the floor. It clattered noisily.

'Giblets!' cried Bonaparte in alarm, squeezing her fingers painfully.

Grace turned on her lamp, and handed it to Bonaparte. In the trembling yellowish light, Grace picked out a curved flat object, greenish, and splotched with yellow and red. It had two hooks on the back.

'I wonder what it's made of,' she said. 'It isn't plastic or metal or wood.'

'A shield I think,' said Bonaparte. 'It could have been made for you. The size is perfect.' Grace found a way of hooking it over her left arm to protect the whole left side of her body. It was surprisingly light.

As you know, Grace was not the sort of person who walked about with a shield. Not many people did in London any more, and it would have seemed *unusual* to take it into school or to the park. In the dark, somewhere deep in the roots of the earth below Yawngrave Tower, however, everything was different. Grace felt immediately that it belonged on her arm.

'I think it suits you,' said Bonaparte peering at her. The red and yellow splotches are nicely Normal.

'I'm going to keep it,' said Grace. 'I will examine it properly once we get out of here.'

'Good idea.'

The air was clearly fresher now. And a trickle of water, which they checked with the red lamp, was heading merrily downhill.

'It must lead somewhere,' said Bonaparte.

They followed the stream, and Grace turned her lamp on, illuminating a gritty floor. 'Look!' she said, pointing. She had noticed white splashes of bird lime on the floor.

'We must be close to an opening,' Bonaparte said excitedly. 'Grace, turn off your torch!'

She obeyed. Their eyes adjusted to the dark again.

'Is that light?' said Bonaparte excitedly.

Sure enough, there was a fold of grey in the black. They hurried towards it.

'Do you hear that?' Bonaparte sounded happier, his dread of the dark lifting.

A burst of birdsong, fluent and beautiful drifted towards them.

'Darkling, I listen!' whispered Bonaparte towards the sound.

Grace had to hurry to keep up with the thin man, who was capering towards the light. They seemed to be approaching the round mouth of a cave, which opened into clear blue sky. Just inside the entrance was a rock ahead, and something upright was propped against it. A gull, which gave a startled Yarp! as it flew off. Two birds with dark eyes hopped away too, swooping out into the sky.

Bonaparte was racing now. The object seemed familiar.

'It has a face!' said Grace.

'Skelton!' cried Bonaparte.

Grace caught up with Bonaparte, out of breath.

The face was similar to Skelton's face, but the body was frozen and rigid.

'Skelton!' Bonaparte backed away from his body. 'No,' he said quietly.

Grace lifted a limp arm. 'Skelton,' she said.

Nothing.

She shook him. Behind her Bonaparte stood frozen with horror.

'You're a strange seabird,' a tiny voice rasped.

'Was that him?' said Bonaparte, unable to believe his ears.

'I think so,' said Grace.

'Thank you... Fly away. Fly away my featherbrained friends,' Skelton mumbled.

'It was him!' said Bonaparte, 'His mouth moved. What did he say?'

'Something about *featherbrains*,' said Grace.

'Charming,' said Bonaparte, trying to sound more light-hearted than he felt. Finding Skelton was proving just as worrying as seeking him. Especially as he was not behaving Normally: he was being unusually quiet.

'Skelton!' Grace was alarmed.

Skelton's head lolled senselessly.

Bonaparte had a brainwave. 'Pies!' he said loudly.

Chapter 24

Yawngrave's Theory of Pies

'Pies?' Skelton's eyes popped open. 'What's wrong with your face, Bonaparte? Am I dead?'

'You don't seem to be, old stick,' said Bonaparte.

'Beaked by dozens of birds, Bonaparte! Hauled into the sky! I'm lucky to be alive,' he said. 'I miss the Island. I miss my mothers too...'

'Mothers?' asked Bonaparte, frowning.

'And here's Grace Brown!' Skelton cried cheerfully, half standing up, before crumpling again. 'My mothers said we were woven together by fate. Is that why you are here?

'No,' said Bonaparte, worriedly hauling his friend to his feet. He waited till Skelton had stopped wobbling before releasing him. 'She was helping me to find an infuriating old popinjay.'

'And we wanted to warn you about Rick,' Grace added. 'He was being controlled by Mrs Bland. But we were too late...'

'Rick!' Skelton passed a hand over his face. 'Yes, that's right. His mother possessed him. A nasty business.'

'How did you escape her?' asked Bonaparte.

'On the back of an enormous snake,' Skelton said. 'Huge it was! Next I fell off it into the sea in a beautiful bay, made my way ashore and climbed to the top of a hill past the talking water and met my three mothers...'

'He's gone raving mad,' Bonaparte muttered to Grace.

'I am not mad,' Skelton said firmly. 'Besides, Grace is carrying one of the serpent's scales.'

'This?' Grace held out her shield in wonder. 'It must have been enormous!'

'Colossal,' said Skelton. 'But Grace, tell me about Rick.'

Grace described how Mrs Bland had puppeted Rick, his fall from the Tower, and how she had talked to the Golden Cockerel.

'The Golden Cockerel! So he wasn't lying about that,' said Skelton. 'Rick said the Golden Cockerel had a message for me which said: *Explore the dark roots of the world to conquer the besiegers.* Did it have a message for you, Grace?' he continued, trying hard to ignore Bonaparte's expression.

'It said *I want you to be angry*,' said Grace. 'I didn't really understand.'

'It's a mysterious being,' said Skelton. He thought for a moment. 'And what did it actually say to the bat boy?'

'I didn't hear it say anything,' said Grace.

'Nothing? Hmm,' said Skelton. 'So he could be lying. But perhaps it spoke to him without words,' he said.

Bonaparte raised his eyebrows, or the bits of his face that should have had eyebrows if they hadn't all fallen out.

'Don't be annoying Bonaparte. Lots of strange things are happening...' Skelton said, beginning to hobble off. 'I will explain. But we have to get back, and fast too.'

'Diana Yellyface,' said Grace, jogging to keep up. 'I think Rick ate her.'

'Rick *what*?' Skelton said, stopping again. 'How do you know?'

'Mrs Bland told me. She was being cruel,' said Grace. 'Also I observed him eating big moths when we escaped from Charcoal House, so I think it may be true.'

'Never trusted him,' Bonaparte muttered.

They set off again, following the red patch of lamplight in silence.

Skelton cleared his throat in a strange way. 'I'd like to say... What I mean is... Thank you for wanting to help me, and come to my rescue. I don't deserve such good friends.'

'Did you bump your head?' asked Bonaparte.

'Why?'

'Well, you are thanking us.'

'I *am* thanking you.' Skelton said. He was running his thumb over the Pin of Knots as he talked. 'I now understand that we are all woven together. I can't go about thinking nothing I do affects other people. So I repeat: Thank you, Grace. Thank you, Bonaparte.'

'You're welcome, Skelton,' said Grace politely, while Bonaparte awkwardly shook his hand, and said it was no more than Skelton would have done for him.

It was Skelton's turn to tell them everything that had happened to him in enormous detail. For a very, very long time. Eventually, he said, 'From this experience I have invented a theory. It is called *Yawngrave's Theory of Pies.*'

'A theory?' said Grace.

'Yes, you brainy girl,' Skelton said, 'and as you ask, I will explain.' Grace did not remember asking, but he had already started. 'Imagine Bonaparte and I are sharing three pies, and I accidentally eat two of them, with some mustard. This will only leave Bonaparte with one pie.'

'I'm finding this easy to imagine. What sort of pies are they?' said Bonaparte.

'Pay attention,' Skelton said. 'They are not real pies, I am using pies as an example. So if I selfishly left only one pie for Bonaparte, he might feel sad and envious.'

Bonaparte grunted.

'My selfishness would almost certainly put Bonaparte into a bad mood. Bonaparte might be excused for taking his bad mood all the way home to his own house. When Norris Ingbert Boris Banquo Larry Egbert Rattus requests a sprinkle of fresh mixed rubbish for his bowl (after asking where Bonaparte has been for the last six weeks) Bonaparte will suddenly remember the pie unfairness. This will cause him to be unusually tetchy with the Normal rat Norris, who will receive only a few measly sprinkles.

'In turn, Norris will be in even more of a ratty mood than usual. He will boof out into the back garden, find a beetle and give it a nip in the leg for no good reason.'

'Um...' said Bonaparte, confused.

'So what I am saying,' said Skelton, 'is that unless you are careful not to be selfish, lots of other people could be affected. Just like that beetle, who had nothing to do with pies, but is now limping.'

'I see,' said Grace. 'You're saying that if you are unfair to someone, they will be unfair to someone else.'

'In a nutshell, yes,' Skelton said. 'Although I preferred my version of it. And of course if you are unfair to everyone, like Mrs Bland seems to be, unhappiness spreads all across the land—'

'Skelton, you old trilobite,' Bonaparte interrupted. 'While you were talking about pies, I couldn't help noticing that your jacket is ripped and flapping at the back, your shoes are scuffed and salt-stained and your trousers have shrunk. As for your shirt and tie...' He shuddered. 'There may be some truth in your wild story. I believe you fell in the sea, for example, but the business of having *three* mothers...' He shook his head.

At this point, Skelton was tempted to say that just because he had invented *Yawngrave's Theory of Pies*, this didn't mean that Bonaparte had to get jealous and start to be annoying. But he held his tongue.

And so an argument did not start. And nobody was cross in the dark. And soon Skelton was thinking about how much his mothers loved him. And how everyone was connected. And how even words led from one thing to another. Especially the word *and*, which is a conjunction. And...

'*Yawngrave's Theory of Pies*, Bonaparte, old friend,' he said. '*Yawngrave's Theory of Pies*.'

The red lamp was failing now, and everyone was hungry and tired by the time they glimpsed the opening into Skelton's hallway about a hundred metres away.

Bonaparte froze.

'What's that?' he hissed.

Close to the doorway was a big lump hanging in the air.

'I don't remember that,' Skelton said.

'Neither do I,' said Bonaparte, 'Grace. Hand me your lamp!'

Grace beamed the last gleams of her yellowing white light into the dark. A large bat-like shape, wrapped in its own wings, was hanging upside down just inside the opening.

Rick.

Remembering how he had been clubbed by the bat boy's wings, Skelton began grinding his teeth. 'Now we have him,' he growled.

'Don't...' began Grace. 'Please don't hurt him...'

Rick stayed where he was as they approached. There was a little light from the open cupboard door. To their dark-adjusted eyes, it was enough to see by.

Grace noticed something dripping from Rick's wings onto the floor underneath.

The boy fell like a dropped cat. He landed on his feet to face them. Grace thought he had shrunk somehow. He was no longer was a vessel of Mrs Bland's power. He was just an angry and despairing boy.

'Rick,' said Grace. 'Is that you?'

'Who else would it be?' The bat boy turned to Skelton coldly. 'I suppose you want your revenge now.'

'There will be no revenge, Rick,' said Skelton. 'I don't think you were responsible for everything you did. I think you are the beetle who was bitten by a rat.'

'You what?' said Rick.

'Skelton!' Bonaparte said. 'Before you start telling him about *Yawngrave's Theory of Pies* can we just get out of the dark. I HATE it.'

Part III

Bone Fire Night

Chapter 25

The winged weakness

Still holding her dragon shield, Grace climbed out of the circular wooden doorway under the stairs. Compared to deep underground, Skelton's kitchen was barely dark at all. Streetlight fell in stripes through the barred downstairs windows.

Usually full of creaks, slamming doors and the inexplicable clanking of chains, tonight Yawngrave Tower was abnormally quiet. All Grace could hear was the soft growl of traffic on London streets, but nothing from inside at all.

She peered through the thickly regrown glass of the front room window. The last pieces of Skelton's entirely Normal orange and purple fencing had been crushed by the grey digger, but the shell of the car remained, and two watchful men were sitting in it. One, with binoculars, instantly spotted Grace. When Skelton and Bonaparte peered out a few seconds later, the man had smartly picked up a big stone and hurled it, with great accuracy, towards Skelton's head. Everyone ducked, but the stone clanged harmlessly from an iron bar protecting the window. The other man immediately began talking on his phone.

'Shall we find the others?' said Grace.

'Exactly what I was going to say,' said Skelton.

The bat boy watched them sourly. 'You lot can. I don't want to,' he said.

'You must come too,' Skelton said, his patience wearing thin.

'Why should I?' said Rick. 'You all hate me. Even the people outside hate me. I'm going back under the stairs.'

'I don't hate you,' said Grace.

'We need to stick together,' said Skelton, more kindly. 'This includes you, Rick.'

'Please, Rick,' said Grace. 'I'm on your side.'

'Nobody's on my side. Don't you understand? Nobody!' His face twisted strangely.

The deep cut on his wing was showing. Skelton did not like seeing blood, especially when it was dripping on his floor. 'Let's be practical. Your wing needs treating,' he said, 'and Tibia is good with wounds.'

'If he's still alive, Skelton,' muttered Bonaparte.

Nobody thanked Bonaparte for this bleak thought as Skelton led them upstairs. There were more stairs than before, and the flight had begun to twist, as if it had ambitions to become a spiral staircase.

'We should be careful,' Bonaparte said. 'We have no idea what to expect.'

'Creeping is called for,' Skelton agreed.

'Whispering too,' said Grace under her breath.

'Yes whispering, creeping and tiptoeing,' Skelton said, advancing cautiously.

Being one of the most Normal houses in London, however, the stairs squeaked and creaked with every step.

'You know what.' Skelton stopped. 'This is my own house and I am not going to creep about. I'm going to proceed as Skelton Yawngrave, Master of Yawngrave Tower.'

He squared his thin shoulders, and Grace held up her dragon shield defiantly. Bonaparte puffed out his chest. The bat boy dawdled behind them.

'Ow!' Bonaparte held out his thumbs.

Grace stifled a scream.

On the staircase, coiled an apparition of vermilion flame. Slowly and sinuously, a face like a Chinese fire dragon flowed towards them. A long semi-transparent body slinked behind it, with a visible black heart throbbing in its chest.

Grace shrank back from the gaping mouth, each long tooth a flame. The dragon's eyes were sickening.

Groping black leeches fingered out from their empty sockets towards Grace's face. She shrank back behind her shield. The words of the Golden Cockerel came to her. *I want you to be angry.* Grace's heart smouldered. Why did she always have to be scared? 'Who do you think you are?' she said, stepping towards the dragon.

'I am Vengeance!' said the fiery beast. 'I fight fire with fire.'

'What do you mean, exactly,' said Grace, 'that your name is Vengeance, or that you want vengeance?'

The dragon flared at Grace, who did not move but instead took a step forward. Was there a shred of doubt in this monstrous figure? The orange flames grew dimmer, and it retreated by inches.

Not for the first time in his life, Skelton did something rash. He sprang forward and plunged his hands into the middle of the beast's fiery chest.

'Skelton!' Bonaparte yelped in fear.

'No heat,' Skelton said. 'It's all show.'

'No!' roared the fire dragon, snapping in the air. Suddenly there was something about the voice...

'Of course. Spoony Kooker? Is that you?' said Skelton wearily. 'Spoony it's me! It's your friends Skelton and Grace and Bonaparte.'

The dragon diminished. 'Spoony Kooker? I suppose I was that spirit. But now I am different.' The dragon shrank into something that was more of a flame than a monster.

'You three I will allow. But who is that with you?'

'It's Rick,' said Grace.

'The MURDERER?' Spoony burst between them like a shower of sparks, lancing towards Rick, who, in shock, tumbled backwards. A ball of ectoplasmic fire and frantic black wingbeats rolled downstairs.

'Enough!' a commanding voice rang out. Skelton was surprised to discover that the voice was his. Perhaps it was because he had been clutching the Pin of Knots in his pocket.

'Spoony Pootus Olly Osgood Kooker stop this instant! You are Warden of Yawngrave Tower, but I am its Master!'

To his astonishment, the fighting stopped.

Tibia and Fibula were asleep in the War Room, curled among empty boxes of provisions, among empty goo crusted buckets and piles of heavy objects ready to rain down on the besieging thugs of the O.P.P. Only a few candles flickered, and they showed there had been little time to waste on keeping the War Room tidy.

'At last,' said Grimsby exhaustedly, keeping watch from a shadow near one of the loopholes. 'They've returned from blooming Narnia.'

'Nice to see you too, Grimsby,' Skelton said, observing the curled-up cats. 'I can't believe these felines are sleeping on the job.'

'Sleeping!' repeated Grimsby in a choked voice.

'You ungrateful creaker...' Fibula, awake now, flared up at Skelton. 'Gone for days!'

'Days? It was only a few hours surely?' Skelton said.

'I don't know about blooming Narnia, but here it was days... You grindbones,' she growled. 'The clock says it's after midnight. These are the early hours of the fifth of November.'

Skelton thought back to meeting his mothers. How the bird had hung in the air, frozen in time. But Bonaparte, Grace and Rick had all been gone for days too. One day, he thought, he would have to explore how time works and build an entirely Normal machine to travel about in it.

What he did next surprised everyone.

I'm sorry, I did not realise,' he went straight across the floor, careful not to fall into the weapon vault, and hugged Grimsby and the cats. It was a bit awkward, at first, because they were still cross, and Fibula's tail took some time before it entirely stopped tetchily twitching. But the Master of Yawngrave Tower's absolute happiness at seeing them eventually melted their resentment.

Rick, however, was received frostily. It seemed that Grimsby, Tibia and Fibula were convinced he had devoured Diana Yellyface in the fog of war, and less sure he had been possessed when he did it.

Nevertheless, Tibia looked carefully at his wound. Under his instruction, Grace washed and bandaged it. She was interested to examine Rick's wings. He had been bleeding lots after Mrs Bland had used them to attack Skelton. They were designed for flight, not to be used as weapons.

Rick barely thanked them for their help. When Grace and Tibia were finished, he gingerly descended a ladder into the food vault. He stayed down there, out of sight, eating hungrily and alone.

Having apologised, Skelton now had a lot of explaining to do. 'We are all woven together,' he said, 'so it is good to explain things.' He told them about his adventures. He also started to tell them about *Yawngrave's Theory of Pies*.

'Thank you, Skelton,' Fibula interrupted rapidly. 'While you were in, what do you call it, Grimsby...?'

'Blooming Narnia,' said Grimsby.

'While you were in *Blooming Narnia*, with your "three mothers" we were on commando raids pouring sugar into petrol tanks, glooping slime onto the heads of thugs, and fighting every day.' Here Fibula took a deep breath. 'So to waltz in here and say we were sleeping on the job is annoying even by your exceptionally high standards, Skelton Yawngrave.'

'I agree,' Skelton said. I am sorry. I apologise without reservation. It was wrong of me.'

The Normal cats seemed suspicious. Grimsby shook his ears.

'That's not the first time he has apologised lately,' said Bonaparte. 'Weird, isn't it?'

'My observation,' said Grace, who was now washing her hands and face in a bucket of water, 'is that Skelton has been changed by everything under the stairs.'

'Interesting, Grace,' said Tibia gravely. 'I think we all have been changed by recent events. Especially poor Spoony. He has been magnificent in battle. His terrifying appearance routed the grey thugs. Now, however, they are getting used to him. It can't last.'

'I have another apology,' said Skelton abruptly. Sometimes I say whatever happens to be in my mouth without thinking about other people first. It's an Achilles heel.'

'What's an Achilles heel?' asked Fibula.

'It's a weakness,' said Bonaparte.

'Skelly,' guffawed Grimsby, 'must have more Achilles heels than a spider.'

'I don't think spiders have heels,' said Bonaparte.

'No they don't,' said Grace, 'at least the ones I have examined. I have studied them under my microscope and their legs have seven segments and their feet have two or three claws at the end of them. But I never noticed heels.'

'No, I've never noticed heels either—' said Fibula, licking her lips. She was fond of spiders.

'I wonder,' Skelton interrupted, 'what Mrs Bland's Achilles heel is?'

'*He'd* know,' said Fibula glaring at the top of the ladder.

They all turned to look at Rick, who was emerging from the food vault with a second jar of locusts, unaware that Spoony Kooker was flowing poisonously up the ladder behind him.

'Stop it, Spoony!' Skelton said sternly.

'None of you care about Diana Yellyface, do you?' Spoony said bitterly.

'I'm sorry, Spoony,' said Grace, drying her hands on her grey dress as the ghoul turned an acid yellow. 'But I don't believe Rick killed Diana Yellyface, I think it was *her.*'

As she spoke, Spoony's ectoplasm rapidly flashed in a confusion of different colours. Rick's sullen expression did not change. The truth was that Grace sounded more sure than she really was. She had seen Rick eating moths. And she did not remember him stopping to ask if they were Normal or not. Could it be, Grace thought, that Diana Yellyface had been just one more sky snack?

'What is your mother's weakness, Rick?' Skelton asked.

The boy shrugged, his leathery wings shifting with his shoulders.

'Speak up Rick,' Skelton said gently.

'How do you know it's me speaking and not her?' Rick snarled.

'Your eyes change, and your voice sounds different,' Grace explained.

'What is your mother's weakness, Rick?' Skelton asked again.

Grace put her hand on Rick's shoulder, and Skelton bent his creaking knees and squatted next to him.

The triangle forms my sisters.
Three corners.
For better or worse, their fate is weaving.

The voices were clear in Skelton's head. His mothers! *The triangle forms.* Surely this meant the sulky boy and the Ordinary girl in pigtails.

'He doesn't have to say,' said Grace suddenly. 'I already know what Mrs Bland's weakness is. It's obvious.'

Rick looked away.

'It's him,' said Grace. 'It's Rick.'

Chapter 26

The liar

Next morning, while the Master of Yawngrave Tower was still sleeping after his journey into the underworld, Mrs Bland was on television. It was 5 November. Tonight would be Guy Fawkes Night.

'I mean Normal people no harm,' she said to the interviewer in her beautiful voice, 'but facts are facts. Normal people have always plotted against us. It's well known that Guy Fawkes, for example, was a Normal terrorist. Tonight we celebrate the foiling of the Gunpowder Plot of 1605 when Guy Fawkes put thirty-six barrels of gunpowder under the Parliament building to blow up the King and all his parliament in one enormous explosion. Luckily his fiendish plan was discovered with moments to spare.'

'So,' the interviewer asked, laughing nervously, 'can Normal people expect fireworks from you?'

Mrs Bland laughed too, but her eyes flashed.

'Unfortunately it is no laughing matter. Right now a rabble of armed Normals have barricaded themselves into a house in west London. This gang attacks passers-by for fun. In London! We can't accept this. This is no better than a twenty-first-century Gunpowder Plot and these Normal terrorists want to destroy us. It's common sense that we have to stop them before they do further damage.'

'On that point,' the interviewer said slickly, 'we have a live link to west London. Can you hear me, Sue?'

All over the country, Yawngrave Tower flashed onto people's screens. It was a mysterious and many-branched building that appeared both ancient and modern at the same time.

'Thanks, Tom. I'm in a helicopter above a residential area of west London,' said the reporter. 'As you can see now on your screen, this bizarre Normal fortification has been constructed with unusual speed. Our pictures show the fire damage done to the area. Notice the burnt-out cars too. Notice a group of brave local people who have assembled outside. They say they want to prevent those inside from making an escape. It's a dangerous stand-off here in west London. It seems Ordinary people are getting big bonfires ready for tonight. Back to you in the studio Tom.'

'What do you make of those pictures, Mrs Bland?'

'It is what you'd expect,' said Mrs Bland. 'As I have said, these Normal people are terrorists, why else would they wall themselves in.'

'But bonfires, Mrs Bland. Why bonfires?'

'We must fight fire with fire, that's why,' she snapped.

'It's just been confirmed,' said the interviewer, 'that this property, if that's the right word, belongs to an individual named Skelton Yawngrave—'

'A notorious plotter,' interrupted Mrs Bland. 'Make no mistake. Yawngrave is pulling the strings. Inside that illegal building is a poor Ordinary girl named Grey Brown, who Yawngrave has brutally kidnapped and is now holding hostage. I have personally spoken to the poor girl's parents, who are sick with worry. We owe it to Ordinary people, like poor darling Grey Brown, not to give in to these fanatics. And as you saw, I've asked volunteers from the O.P.P. to keep watch on Yawngrave's hateful mob. Brave O.P.P. members are standing up for every Ordinary person in this country.'

Mr Grayling could hear the news helicopter hovering above him through the roof of the white van parked a few streets away from Yawngrave Tower. He had just swapped his grey business suit and tie for jeans and a hoodie. Before he stepped out of the back of the van, he examined one last time the explosives strapped to a wooden pallet and sealed in plastic.

'They'll wish it was just thirty-six barrels of gunpowder,' he said to the driver through a metal grille. 'What we have here is enough high explosive to launch Yawngrave Tower into space. And take all the Normals with it.' The driver laughed. 'Sends a message, Patel, loud and clear across the country: no Normal trouble will be tolerated.'

He climbed out of the back of the van and locked it. The driver, Patel, opened his window so Grayling could speak to him.

'Stay here,' said Grayling. 'I'll message you when it is time to wrap the present up nicely.'

'Okay, boss,' said Patel, his eyes shining with eagerness, 'can't wait.'

'Good man. And the other van?' Grayling stopped for a moment.

'On its way sir. Three Normals inside.'

'Excellent.' Grayling stretched his thin lips into a smile. 'Oh, and one more word, Patel.'

'Yes sir?'

'Boom!' Grayling said.

The street seemed empty. As Grayling set off for Yawngrave Tower no cars were parked nearby. The tarmac was scorched and melted. Further down the street mysterious roadworks had sprung up, blocking any traffic. Nobody would enter this street tonight, unless the O.P.P. allowed them to.

When he approached Skelton Yawngrave's home, however, he was surrounded by party members who were gathered outside, eager for instructions.

'Tonight's the night,' Grayling said to them. 'Mrs Bland will be here in person to make sure Guy Fawkes Night is remembered for a new reason.' There was a cheer, and some clapping. Grayling glanced at a message on his phone. 'Now if you'll excuse me… Keep up the good work, everyone. Keep building the bonfires. Let's make tonight a night to remember. Ordinary is as Ordinary does!'

The crowd dispersed to a safe distance from the Tower, loitering in knots of two and three. Others hurried over to where great pyramids of firewood were being constructed.

Grayling walked back to see a second white van pull up behind the first. The driver handed him some keys, and a plastic bag. Grayling walked to the back of the van, which was old and dented, unlocked the door and stepped inside.

Half the van had been converted into a cage. Behind the bars, three Normal children sat cowering in the corner; twin boys and their older sister. The girl glared at Grayling with the ice-blue eyes of a wolf.

Mr Grayling pulled out some small plastic bottles of water, and some chocolate from the plastic bag. But he did not hand them over.

'Do you remember what you were told you to do?' he asked quietly.

'Yes,' said the girl, 'we do, sir.'

'Good girl,' said Grayling, poking the plastic bottles through the bars. Warily the girl took the water and then the chocolate. Her brothers tore off the wrapping hungrily, because everyone, Normal or Ordinary, loves chocolate.

'But why do we have to do it?' asked the one of the boys. Both twins had the unusually hairy faces of werewolves.

'You really are quite stupid, aren't you,' said Grayling coldly. 'We have your hideous parents. Handing over a present isn't too much to repay Mrs Bland for keeping them safe, is it?'

The girl tried to speak again, but Grayling was already slamming the van door, and locking the children inside.

'Special delivery?' he muttered. Then he repeated the phrase several times, chuckling to himself.

Chapter 27

Four into three

Despite the insistent clatter of a news helicopter overhead, Skelton still managed to sleep peacefully on his temporary bed hooks the War Room.

Nearby, Tibia and Grimsby (who had woken everyone up in the middle of the night by shouting *don't leave me alone!* in his sleep) were fitfully dozing. Rick remained curled up with his wings tight about him, despite one being bandaged. He had not spoken to anyone since last night.

Grace was awake. She had slept happily through the night wrapped up in blankets in a comfortable bubble shaped room just off the war room. Bonaparte had insisted on putting her grimy and blood stained clothes in the clothes washer overnight and had dried them so she could wear them fresh in the morning. He said the O.P.P. grey might help to keep her safe *if anything happened*.

Grace had slept by the curved wall, but now, getting out of her nest of blankets she stood in the middle of the little room. Here the wood of the floor became spongy and her feet sank in a little. As soon as she did so, little holes opened overhead. A soft and wonderfully refreshing shower fell on her. The water in her mouth was both sweet and mineral, and lathered naturally in her hair. This tower – *or tree?* she thought – was full of surprises.

Grace, now clean and dressed and carrying her shield, joined Bonaparte who was keeping watch through a loophole in the War Room. Nervously, they observed O.P.P. members, forming a human chain. Along it they now passed pieces of smashed up Normal furniture from hand to hand. Brightly coloured wardrobes, tables, chairs, even floorboards were flung onto to the ground to create hill of wood was now twice the height of a man. It appeared that they had looted Normal houses to find all this wood.

'It's bonfire night, and I think they still want to burn me, Bonaparte,' whispered Grace, not wanting to disturb the others dozing in the war room behind them.

'Cheer up, Grace Brown,' Bonaparte murmured. Then he grinned at her ruefully, as he found he had nothing cheerful to say.

'Bonaparte,' Grace said slowly, pulling her head back into the shadow. 'I'm not a witch just because they *say* I'm a witch, am I?'

'People see what they want to see, Grace Brown. If they want to see you as a witch, they will. Just as if they want to see me and Skelton as walking skeletons, instead of extremely thin people, they do.'

'So I'm not a witch, then?'

Bonaparte shrugged. 'You might well be a witch, you young whippersnapper. But, if you are a witch, make sure that it is something you choose for yourself, not something someone tells you to be.'

Grace was puzzled. 'How can I *choose* to be a witch? Surely I'm either a witch or I'm not a witch. A false widow spider doesn't choose to be false widow spider. It's just born that way.'

'But unlike one of those nippy arachnids, you have to make your own decisions, Grace Brown,' said Bonaparte. 'Your brain is a bit more complicated.'

This was a fact, but Grace was still thoughtful.

'If I *could* choose to be a witch, does that mean Mrs Bland has won? Have I turned into what Mrs Bland wanted me to be?'

Bonaparte shrugged.

'I don't know. You just have to be yourself' – he gave a crooked smile – 'whatever that is Grace Brown. Sometimes you have to do what you can to survive.'

They put their faces next to the loopholes again. The sunset turned their faces golden and orange.

A few streets away, in a shaded garden, a shower of yellow sparks fizzed in the half light. A Catherine wheel was twisting on its nail. Two bangers cracked on the street outside. Soon the sky would be alive with thunderclaps, explosions and shrieking rockets. For it was 5 November: Guy Fawkes' Night.

'First helicopters, now fireworks,' said Tibia crossly, uncurling from his catnap, 'the perfect cover to do us harm.'

'Listen! That rotten digger is back!' called Fibula, suddenly wide awake with her ears pricked.

Soon the others could hear a heavy machine rumbling along the street towards them. Without pausing, the mechanical digger clanked straight up into the front garden.

'What's that thing?' asked Grace, alarmed.

'It seems they have found a vintage wrecking ball,' said Tibia in dismay. The machine had now been armed with a great iron ball on the end of a chain. It was spiked like a giant medieval mace.

The crowd began to chant as if they were at a football match.

'What are they saying?' said Skelton in a thick voice, reluctantly unhooking his arms from his sleeping hooks.

'*Knock-knock! Knock-knock!*' said Fibula.

'Brace yourselves! Now!' Tibia shouted.

A great boom, and a scrunch of tortured wood and squealing stone echoed around them. Yawngrave Tower staggered on its foundations.

'*Who's there?*' cried the crowd.

Skelton was wide awake now. 'What's happening?' he asked.

'Almost breached the wall by the sound of it!' said Tibia.

'The defences!' roared Grimsby. He, with Skelton and Bonaparte, who had both rushed to help, pulled the levers to release gallons of slime. It slopped down onto the destructive machine, smearing the windscreen of driver's cabin. Two O.P.P. members slipped over in the stinking goo.

Spoony Kooker who had been flitting endlessly from room to room downstairs, billowed out through the front door at them. This time, however, instead of everyone turning to flee in terror of his awful shrieks, nobody moved.

One man simply pointed and sniggered. Grace saw two young women turn their backs to take selfies with Spoony over their shoulders in the background.

'They're mocking him!' Skelton said. The ghoul wilted noticeably in the air.

'*Knock-knock*! *Knock-knock*!' the crowd chanted.

Another crunching thud. But this time, the blow was slightly off target, only scuffing the Tower. The engine of the great machine was coughing. Even if Spoony was no longer useful, the foul slime was doing its work, oozing into the great engine of the digger.

'*Who's there? Who's there?*' the crowd called. The machine growled and choked more, and stalled. The next crushing hit did not come.

Outside someone was trying to light the big fire.

'Oh Mothers, what should we do?' Skelton said aloud.

Three fates must weave.

Mother Urth, The Weaver of Fate, had answered him. Skelton knew that whatever the solution was, it involved Grace and Rick somehow.

'If Rick is Mrs Bland's weakness, whatever that means,' Bonaparte said, 'I suggest you use him now, old chum. Perhaps he can interfere with her plans.'

'You're right Bonaparte,' Skelton said slowly, 'let's put her off her stroke.' As he had fiddled nervously with the Pin of Knots in his pockets a brilliant idea had whooshed into his brainbox. Now it fanned out like a peacock's tail and strutted about. 'Listen! We're all connected, that's what my mother said—'

'Okay,' Bonaparte rolled his eyes, a move he had copied from Grace.

'Harken Bonaparte! If Mrs Bland can speak to us through Rick...'

'We can give *her* a call back, *through* Rick,' finished Grace.

'Indeed my girl. A nuisance call when she's least expecting it,' said Skelton, delighted that the same brilliant idea had struck Grace too. 'But what are we going to say?'

'Hello!' said Rick. 'I'm here too. I'm a person not a thing.'

'The only person who treats you like a *thing* is your mother,' said Grace.

'No, *all* of you do,' Rick flared. 'I'm sick of you lot. You think I'll go off like a bomb when my mother presses the trigger.'

Nobody said anything.

'See!' said Rick.

'You can't help having Mrs Bland as your mother,' said Skelton.

'Oh shut up,' said Rick, 'what do you know about it? You fool. Prancing about in your stupid clothes. You're nothing but a glutton who makes everyone feel sick just to watch you eat. You're a stupid stinking skeleton who—'

The bat boy reeled, clutching the side of his head. Bonaparte had slapped him.

'Bonaparte! I have very mixed feelings—' Skelton said.

'Don't do that again, Bonaparte,' shouted Grace angrily. 'It means we are just as bad as Mrs Bland.'

'I couldn't help myself,' said Bonaparte. He soon felt ashamed, however, and apologised. Rick glared venomously at him in response.

'They are lighting the big bonfire!' shouted Tibia. 'Don't just stand there!'

'Please help them, Bonaparte,' Skelton said, twisting the woven gold triangle in his pocket. 'I must...'

Walk through the weird door.

The voice of his Mother Urth came to Skelton again.

'I must walk through the weird door,' Skelton said.

'What weird door?' asked Grace.

As if in answer, there came a tentative creak, followed by an ear-splitting squeal that made her wince. Immediately behind them in the wall of the War Room, a new door had dragged itself open to reveal a secret chamber.

'Ah-ha!' said Skelton. 'This has been woven already. Is this weird enough for you, Grace? Come on!' Trusting his mothers, he entered, and Grace followed, holding her shield tightly.

'That's right,' Grimsby called after them, 'disappear again just when you're needed why don't you!'

'I'm with you, Grimsby,' said Bonaparte, and they hurried off.

Grace followed Skelton into what was a very Normal room, with three walls. In its centre was a raised three-sided plinth of polished black stone, carved with intertwined snakes. There was nowhere else to stand, so Grace stood on one side of the triangular plinth.

'This must be where the threads meet,' Skelton said, standing on another side.

Rick wavered in the doorway.

'Rick, we need your help,' said Skelton.

'Oh do you?' said Rick. 'Who do you think you are, ordering me about?'

'Don't you see? This is about who *we* are together,' said Skelton.

Almost despite himself, Rick entered and he took a place on the third side of the plinth.

'How can we make her come?' asked Grace, realising what Skelton planned.

'Trust me,' Skelton said.

'D'uh!' said Rick. 'I don't trust you. I don't trust *anyone*! You treat me like a criminal. You all do,' he said, with a spiteful look at Grace. 'Don't you realise?

You can't *make* my mother do anything. You can't just summon her like a servant.'

'Let me show you this,' Skelton said, taking the Pin of Knots from his pocket.

Grace gazed at the triangle within a triangle. The golden pattern had no end, and no beginning. She felt it was a like a map of paths that she must explore or else her life would be sad and shrunken. Rick seemed spellbound too, but fought not to show it.

'It's a symbol,' Skelton continued. 'The centre came from my father, the rest was from my mothers. As far as I understand, it expresses how we are all woven together. *Especially* the three people in this room.'

Skelton rested his hand on the top of the plinth, so the children could better see the Pin of Knots. At that moment, the plinth's stone snakes hissed. Three miniature trapdoors opened on the flat top, and equally miniature clamps sprang clear of the jet black stone, forming a triangular housing. Skelton, with several misgivings (despite his trust in his mothers) dropped the Pin of Knots into the place that had been so clearly designed for it.

There was a crackle. Something like static electricity made the strands of Grace's hair (that weren't in pigtails) rise up from her head.

'I summon Ann Bland,' said Skelton hoarsely. He nodded at Grace to do the same.

'Er. I summon Ann Bland,' said Grace.

'I summon...' Rick groaned. His eyes rolled back so that only the whites showed. His body jerked and trembled, green fire electrified his irises. 'How dare you?' The dreadful eyes focused. 'Yawngrave! And the little witch!'

Now the gaze settled on the Pin of Knots.

'What is that?' There was harshness in Mrs Bland's voice as she saw the woven triangle. Rick's rigid body lurched back.

'Something from my mothers. Something from my father,' Skelton said.

'Fool! Tell me what that *thing* is!'

'Don't call him a fool!' said Grace, her voice choked with anger. 'You horrible bully! We don't have to do what you tell us!'

Skelton held up his hand.

'Grace, I will explain. You see, madam, this is a symbol of how we three are woven together. I believe that we can draw out the good in you that has been long buried.'

Skelton's finger was magnetised to the woven triangle of the Pin of Knots. He slid his finger over the top of it, now housed in the smooth black stone.

Enter a place without time Skelton.

Everything slowed as it had done when he saw the mothers. To Skelton, Grace and Rick appeared to be frozen. In the synapses of his own brain, however, connections fired and information flowed. Again Grace reminded him forcibly of Sunny Applebiter Dolmalus. Sunny had been like a sister to him.

Time slurred to a stop. Skelton saw Rick's invaded body, with Mrs Bland's emerald glint flickering in his eyes.

In that moment well over one hundred years evaporated. Skelton was standing in the centre of a playground full of puddles in *Ye Normal School for Young Gentlefolk.*

Remember... Remember... The fifth of November. He heard children's voices singing. His classmates.

Someone was recklessly throwing fireworks. What was that shouting? Was there a fight in the playground?

There was Sunny! Unmistakable. She was surrounded by chanting children.

You're not Normal. You're Ordinary.

I am a witch! A Normal witch!

It doesn't matter. You don't look like us. You're so Ordinary.

Leave me alone, you fool!

Don't call me a fool!

Skelton! Skelton, help me! He hit me!

'I know who you are.' Skelton said, but he was standing outside time. His voice was unheard. Then lifted his finger from the pin, and time staggered back. He snapped back into the present moment and Grace and Rick breathed again. He gazed into the green eyes he had once known so well.

'I name you Sunny Applebiter Dolmalus,' Skelton said pointing a white knuckled finger at the body possessed by Mrs Bland. His voice shook.

Grace had never seen this expression on Skelton's face.

'What's wrong, Skelton?' she asked.

Skelton shook his head. A teardrop was falling from the corner of his left eye.

'Sunny is dead,' said Mrs Bland, flatly.

'But who *is* Sunny?' Grace said.

'She is. She is Sunny,' Skelton said.

'You know me at last, Skelton.' Mrs Bland laughed again. 'The fool loved me once. In a different century and a different world.'

'What happened to you?' Skelton said.

'Sunny is dead! Normal people, like you, killed Sunny. Now I'm Ordinary, with two Ordinary children. Except for this wretch, my first-born shame!'

Rick's body shook, his arm jerked towards the pin. Fiercely, Skelton was able to hold it back until Rick's body slackened again.

'When I look at you, Skelton, all I see is weakness. When I hear you I hear every single rudeness, feel every blow Normals rained down on me.'

'But I always tried to help you, you know I did—' Skelton said in a broken voice.

'So, you hate Normal people. But you hate Ordinary people too,' Grace broke in angrily. 'You attack Normal people and enslave Ordinary people. Why don't you leave everyone alone?'

'Alone?' Mrs Bland laughed coldly. 'But everyone's alone now. Forever! And now that they are alone, I can rule them. Am I not extraordinary, Grace Brown? You know this.'

'No!' Skelton shouted. 'No! We are all woven together, Normal and Ordinary. We are all in the same web! Sunny, you can stop this. I know somewhere inside you beats a true heart.'

Madness tainted Mrs Bland's laugh.

'No *heart*, Skelton. Not any more. Don't you see I can only be invincible when you're gone? All my weaknesses must be deleted.' Her green eyes blazed from Rick's face. 'And you thought this boy was my weakness?' Rick's body shook. 'Hysterical!'

'I won't let you delete us!' Grace blazed with anger.

'Won't you, girl?' Mrs Bland sneered at Grace. 'I am outside your walls, Yawngrave. Those spellbound grey fools will do anything I say. They will destroy your Tower. What a bonfire there will be. Cats and dogs and girls and boys and skeletons all burning. All burning... Burning... Burning. Every weakness gone.' Mrs Bland's voice trailed off into a strange sing-song. 'Your time is coming, witch girl—'

'Shut up!' Grace shouted. 'I break this! I'm ending the call!

She banged her dragon shield into poor Rick's body. He crumpled to the ground. Mrs Bland was gone. Grace had dismissed her.

'How did you do that?' Skelton said, amazement in his voice.

'I got angry,' said Grace.

Almost silently, the tiny clamps released the Pin of Knots. Skelton snatched it back, relieved.

With Grace's help, he pulled Rick from the weird room.

'Skelton! Come on!' It was Grimsby. He sounded desperate.

'I'm coming,' Skelton said, quietly, but he did not move.

Rick sprang to his feet, having returned to himself. 'Idiots!' he shouted. Before anyone could react, he bolted for a spiral staircase and disappeared up it, his feet rattling on the stairs as he climbed. Eventually he reached a trapdoor and scrambled out onto the turret.

From this height he surveyed the Tower, the streets of London and the fire below.

Night had just fallen. A rocket exploded thunderously nearby. The sky was already full of sparks.

'Idiots everywhere,' he said.

Downstairs, Skelton sank to his knees and covered his face.

'Skelton? What's wrong?' said Grace.

'I can't fight her any more,' Skelton said. 'Sunny was like a sister to me. I loved her.'

'There's no time for this, Skelton. They're firing rockets!' yelled Tibia in alarm. They could hear the whoosh of fireworks shooting up into the branches of the Tower. Incendiary sparks showered everywhere.

'You may not have to fight her, Skelton lad,' said Grimsby. 'Something blinking brilliant is happening; they're reversing the digger. It's driving off!'

Chapter 28

The gift bearers

'Mrs Bland? Mrs Bland?' Grayling leant over the leader of the O.P.P, an anxious expression on his face. He had ordered the digger to retreat. Now, stepping into the limousine he discovered Mrs Bland lying limply on the back seat, only the whites of her eyes showing. Was she... Dead?

'Mrs Bland! Please! Are you okay?'

'Woven together...' she murmured. A spasm gripped her, twitching her rigidly upright. 'I am fine,' she gasped.

'Are you sure?' asked Grayling, his voice still anxious.

'I tell you I am fine,' she snapped. 'Some Normal trickery of Yawngrave's, that's all. The sooner we clear this rats' nest, the better.'

'Can I show you our tame Normals?' Grayling asked eagerly, pointing across the road. 'They're in that van.'

Mrs Bland nodded curtly, and stepped out of the car when Grayling opened her door. The street was empty of other vehicles. The O.P.P. had seen to that. They walked across to the van, and Grayling opened its back door.

Inside, the caged children were still huddled together. The girl stared warily with her blue wolf eyes.

'You,' Mrs Bland snapped. 'What do they call you? And I don't want the full Normal name, just your first name.'

'Hortense,' said the girl. 'And this is Victor and this is Viking, they are—'

Grayling laughed coldly. 'That's enough,' he said.

'Listen to me, Hortense, let me remind you that I can delete your parents like *that*, if I feel like it.' Mrs Bland thrust her arm through the bars and snapped her fingers in the girl's face. 'Do your job, and they might survive. So let me repeat, your simple task is to deliver this present to Skelton Yawngrave. All you do is walk up to the door and knock on it. The people inside will see that you are Normal, and invite you in. Give them the parcel, and this message: "This a gift from Ordinary people everywhere." Do you think you can do that?'

Hortense nodded, but Mrs Bland made her repeat the message three times. The boys watched Mrs Bland meekly, not daring to speak.

'Mr Grayling' – Mrs Bland had turned to him now – 'has the present been wrapped?'

'Yes it has,' said Grayling.

'And will it be a proper surprise when they open it?'

'Oh yes. Very surprising,' said Grayling. He opened the back door, and whistled. Two men handed him a heavy parcel. He laid it carefully just inside the van. 'Mustn't damage the present,' he said.

Grayling called out *drive!* and the van edged ahead, turning a corner and proceeding slowly down the street for thirty seconds.

'We're here, ma'am,' shouted the driver.

Mrs Bland, warning the children with her eyes, stepped out from the battered van. There was a shout of delight, followed by cheering and applause. Mrs Bland had surprised her army of grey-clad followers outside Yawngrave Tower.

By the time the applause died down, Grayling had released the Normal children from the cage in the van. They stepped out into the centre of a crowd that had gathered around their leader. Someone spat on Viking's legs.

Mrs Bland held up her hand. The crowd hushed.

'I see the area has been cleared,' she said. For the digger had retreated. All vans, apart from the one she had just stepped out from, had been driven away. 'Well done, everyone. Nothing here now, but us, this fire and our fireworks.

'These *unusual* children are here to help us. Now children, pick up the present as you were told,' she said, her voice honey-sweet.

With difficulty, Hortense and her brothers lifted the package, which had been neatly wrapped in grey paper.

'Please deliver it to Mr Yawngrave as we agreed,' said Mrs Bland, pointing at Skelton's front door about twenty metres away.

As they walked slowly forward, Yawngrave Tower loomed reassuringly over them. The ground was slippery with goo but, holding onto one another while they carried the parcel, the children managed to keep their feet.

Outside the house, they put the present down. The crowd was silent as Hortense reached up to the door's heavy knocker. She smiled as she avoided the nicely Normal teeth of the bat-faced door knocker, and banged on the door.

'Knock-knock!' said a man in the crowd. The tension broke, and everyone laughed.

There was no answer.

Hortense peeked back at Mrs Bland to see if she should return to her, but the politician's steely expression left her in no doubt.

Eventually Hortense heard the sound of rattling chains, and the sliding of bolts, and of keys turning in locks.

The door opened. Hortense and her brothers saw revealed a kindly and Normal skeleton man. Just behind him, Hortense glimpsed a girl of about her own age, who had a serious face and carried what seemed to be a shield.

'Come in, children, I'm Skelton Kirkley Elvis Lupus Lionel Yawngrave III, and you are very welcome.'

Hortense glanced back at the silent grey crowd, and the evil woman.

Gratefully, the three children stepped into Yawngrave Tower, and Skelton Yawngrave bolted the door behind them.

Standing outside, Grayling shouted at people. 'Move back! Move away from the house! Run! Take cover!'

He slapped the side of the van, and its driver sped it away down the street.

The excited crowd scattered, ducking down behind garden walls and around the corner of the street, or pressing themselves behind trees.

Thirty seconds, from... Now!' said Grayling, pressing something on his smartphone's screen. 'Then it will all be over.'

30 'Welcome,' said Skelton.

29 Hortense saw Grace

28 peering at her over a colourful shield.

27 Grace smiled. 'Hello,' she said.

26 Hortense smiled back.

25 Skelton cleared his throat,

24 'Now, you young

23 pipsqueaks,

22 what's that thing

21 you're carrying?'

20 'It's a present,' said Hortense,

19 'from Mrs Bland.

18 She told us to say

17 it is a gift from

16 Ordinary people

15 everywhere.'

14 'Boom' said Victor, one of the twins.

13 'Boom?' said Skelton.

12 'I heard Mr Grayling

11 say "boom",' said Victor.

10 Skelton picked up the package.

9 'Help me!' he shouted, running towards the cupboard under the stairs.

8 'Open it!' he roared at Bonaparte.

7 'I'm trying,' said Bonaparte.

6   Bonaparte pulled at the bolts on the round door.

5   'Hurry!' yelled Skelton.

4   'I'm TRYING!' yelled Bonaparte.

3   The round door sprang open.

2   Skelton and Bonaparte flung the parcel inside.

1   Bonaparte slammed the round door shut.

BOOOOOOOOOOOOOOOOOOOOOOOM!

'We should all be dead by now,' said Bonaparte, after the floor had stopped shaking. Everyone picked themselves up. Above them, Yawngrave Tower was still standing, but it shuddered and creaked like a tree in a gale.

The bomb's force had been released in the empty darkness below, but the streets around them felt as if they were trembling.

Skelton was laughing.

'She's slipping! She knows I have an enormous cavern under my house,' said Skelton. 'She's not as smart as we think she is.'

'She didn't realise you could think so fast,' said Grace.

Grimsby and the cats bounded downstairs.

'What the blooming heck was that?' asked Grimsby.

'A bomb. Mrs Bland told these three poor children to bring it indoors,' said Skelton.

'We chucked it in the cupboard under the stairs,' Bonaparte added. 'Plenty of room down there for bombs.'

'Good thinking!' said Tibia.

'You deserve a medal for sticking it down there, Skelly,' Grimsby said.

The wolf children stood in silence, not knowing what to do or say.

Grace walked over to Hortense, Victor and his twin, Viking, and hugged them.

'How did she make you do it?' Grace asked.

'They've imprisoned our parents,' said Hortense. 'They said they would kill them. Honestly, we didn't know it was a bomb.'

'A Trojan horse. An old trick,' said Bonaparte sadly. 'It's hard to imagine that even Mrs Bland could use children to deliver a gift stuffed full of explosives.' He said sternly.

'Bonaparte, I don't like the way you are looking at me,' said Skelton.

'Don't tell me now that you *still* love this woman?' said Bonaparte.

Chapter 29

Decision time

Rapidly, Fibula and Grimsby fed and washed the three wolf-children. This done, they led them into the bubble-shaped chamber near the War Room where Grace had slept last night. Here Hortense, Victor and Viking, who had been exhausted by their horrible experience, were soon curled fast asleep and safe in the heart of the Tower.

The others gathered in the War Room. Even Spoony Kooker was there, lurking like a great candle flame in a shadowy corner. Rick had not returned from the upper floors.

'We'll talk to those poor were-children again when they've rested,' Skelton said.

'They are more proof that the Sunny you loved no longer exists, Skelton,' said Grace, even though the thin man clearly didn't want to talk about it. 'Sunny would never have used innocent children to try to murder you.'

'Of course not,' said Skelton, 'but a century isn't a long time when you love somebody.'

'It is a long time to love someone who can't love you back,' said Grace.

Skelton listened to her in wonder. 'You are an extraordinary person,' he said eventually. 'What are you? Eleven? You have a wise head on your shoulders, Grace Brown.'

Listen to the girl! It is fated for you to resist Ann Bland, even if you have to fight your own heart too.

Three voices in unison. Skelton's mothers were unanimous.

A trapdoor flipped open in Skelton's mind, and a new thought bounced blinking into the light. Act now, said the thought, and *Be sure to dress your best.*

Skelton strode to the War Room's emergency wardrobe. He changed his jacket to a fine one of rich purple velvet, and selected scarlet trousers with a single fine purple stripe running down the side. From the small collection of fifteen hats, he selected his highest top hat and balanced it on his head. He chose an orange tie, and he pinned this into place on his shirt with the triangle of woven gold.

'It *is* important to dress with dignity,' he muttered to himself. He picked a minute piece of lint from his sleeve, with a tut.

'Skelton, what are you up to?' asked Bonaparte suspiciously.

'The final touch,' he said, reaching into the armoury. 'Here it is: *the Skullcruncher*, my trusty cutlass. It is time.'

The others began to gather about him.

'We've warned you about that weapon,' growled Tibia. 'Put it down.'

'It is time, Tibia, my dear comrade,' Skelton said. 'I must personally face the enemies at my door. I must do it alone too.'

'Alone? That's just barking mad, you troubling bunion,' said Bonaparte, aghast.

Skelton touched the woven triangle on his chest and drew strength from it.

'It is time,' he said.

'Will you stop saying that!' said Bonaparte irritably.

Skelton now strode downstairs. Bonaparte, Tibia, Fibula, Grimsby and Grace followed. They were all arguing with him at once (while keeping a safe distance from the cutlass).

Skelton did not reply. He paused to enjoy his favourite completely Normal cold and clammy spot in the hallway. He adjusted the angle of his top hat for the third or fourth time in the refreshing cool.

Grimsby flattened his broad back against the front door.

'We can't let you out there, Skelly,' said the Normal dog.

'It is time,' Skelton said once more. All the conversations about chewed fences he was thinking of having with Grimsby were forgotten. 'Thank you, Grimsby. As you know, I am the Master of Yawngrave Tower. My friends have suffered too long. Sometimes you have to do what you can. You can't just hole up in your Tower forever, waiting for something to happen. Sometimes you have to make it happen.'

'You brain-free popinjay,' said Bonaparte. 'What is your *plan*? They might kill you. They probably *will* kill you if you just walk out there.'

In reply, Skelton touched the woven triangle on his chest.

'I trust my magnificent mothers. I trust old Pop Yawngrave. Perhaps,' he added with a sigh, 'I'll see him again soon.'

'You were just going out without saying goodbye?' said Fibula, sleeking forwards. Tibia also pushed his battered head at Skelton. Skelton went down on his knees and was briefly allowed to scratch them both behind their ears.

'Farewell, felines,' he said fondly.

'You old creaker,' said Fibula sadly.

Skelton was trying not to look at Grace's face. Sometimes it moved too much. He did not want to see the tears dripping from her eyes, even though she was trying to hide them behind her shield.

Skelton cleared his throat.

'Bonaparte old chum, Spoony, Fibula, Tibia, Grimsby and Grace,' Skelton said. 'As Master of Yawngrave Tower, I leave you with this recommendation. If anything happens to me, you must escape under the stairs. The grey mob not follow you there. And if they *do* kill me… Well nowhere else in London will be safe for Normal people. I go outside because I will not have everyone else exposed to unnecessary danger. Even if we all went outside, we could not defeat them by violence.'

'But what is your *plan*?' wailed Bonaparte. 'You can't go out without a *plan*.'

'I am going to speak the truth. I am going out with the plan of standing up to them. I...' Skelton knew he was not being clear. 'I know it's hard, Bonaparte, but this is just something I have to do. It is something that was woven into my life from the day I was born. For I am Skelton Kirkley Elvis Lionel Lupus Yawngrave III. And as Master of Yawngrave Tower I order you to stay inside.'

Of course everyone started arguing again. Skelton put up his hand, which held the woven gold. With some ceremony, he pinned the Pin of Knots back onto his tie.

'Sometimes we must do things we don't understand,' said Spoony, surprising everyone. 'You should stand up for what you love, and what you know to be true, even if you don't have a plan.' The ghoul's sad underwater face, his colours shifting, made him appear like a kind of subtle cuttlefish.

'Well said, Spoony Kooker, Warden of Yawngrave Tower. Will you promise me, on your word of honour, that you won't follow me even if you want to? I am Master, but you are Warden. You must oversee my ancestors, and make sure that what remains of me is collected to join the others.'

'You have my word,' said Spoony.

Skelton turned to the door and opened it, listening with appreciation one last time to its Normal creak. It did Yawngrave Tower proud.

A war-like clamour rose to meet Skelton.

'Goodbye,' he said. He stepped out into the cacophonous firelight, knowing that nothing would ever be the same again.

Behind Skelton, the whole Tower gave a shudder, like a giant about to wake from centuries of sleep. *Another* transformation? Bonaparte and the mob turned to see what was happening above the door.

In that same split second, quick as a bird, Grace, darted outside after Skelton.

'No!' Bonaparte called, but in lunging after her, he almost lost his arm. For, with an iron shriek, a great portcullis stabbed down from above, protecting the entrance to Yawngrave Tower behind a latticed grille of steel.

'Grace! Skelton!' called Bonaparte desperately, his mouth pressing through the metal. Fibula tried to squeeze between the gaps in the portcullis, but her head was just too big. She, Tibia, Grimsby and Bonaparte now watched their friends helplessly.

The bonfire was blazing dangerously. Grace could feel the heat on her face, yet still the O.P.P. fed the flames. Perched on top of the bonfire was a skeletal figure. It was an effigy of Skelton, and fire was already licking its boots.

The air smelt of gunpowder and was full of explosions: the bangers and jumping jacks the crowd began throwing towards Grace and Skelton; the rockets that screeched into the sky overhead to explode among the turrets of Yawngrave Tower.

Skelton, the real Skelton, stood before her. His left hand was clenched on his chest, over the woven gold of the Pin of Knots. In his right hand, was his dangerous cutlass, which he flailed wildly. At one point he almost knocked his own hat off. More than a dozen men, armed with knives and hammers and heavy steel spanners and crowbars began to surround him. He didn't stand a chance.

'Stop!' Mrs Bland's order rang out above the noise. 'Let the cat play with the mouse.'

The crowd came back to heel, although it was still maddened and straining at the leash. They yelled obscenities about stinking bones and Normals. More fireworks were chucked at Skelton. One bounced, with a spurt of sparks, from the top of his top hat.

'Dance, you freakshow!'

But Skelton would not dance.

Chapter 30

Bone Fire Night

Now the camera lenses were all trained on Grace, walking into the fray to join Skelton. Mrs Bland hated it. Images of this Ordinary girl, behind a Normal shield, would soon be on every screen in the country and spreading virally around the world. What message would an Ordinary girl and a Normal skeleton man standing shoulder to shoulder against her give to her people?

The crowd parted, and Mrs Bland stepped into the firelight. She saw how the cameras were drawn to her again, and how followers raised their phones to film her. Two or three photographers were even scuffling with each other to get the best shot.

Mr Grayling stood behind her watchfully. His right hand was clenched in his pocket.

Mrs Bland had entered the crowd, which parted respectfully for her. The politician grasped the arm of a woman and pulled her free of the throng

With a cruel smile, Mrs Bland shoved the woman in the small of her back, making her step unsteadily towards Grace.

'A reunion. How sweet,' said Mrs Bland.

The bonfire snapped and crackled angrily.

'Mum!' cried Grace in a wounded voice.

'Well, go on,' called Mrs Bland, 'greet your daughter.'

Jerking forwards, Grace's mother was almost in touching distance. 'I...I...' Her face twisted with effort.

'Do go on,' said Mrs Bland.

Grace saw her mother's eyes were vacant. Then they flickered green.

'You disgust me, Grey,' she said. 'You Normal-lover.'

Mrs Bland laughed, Mrs Brown's eyes went blank again.

'Mum…' said Grace.

'Mrs Brown,' said Skelton clearly. 'Can you hear me? The truth is that you are not yourself. You are being controlled by Mrs Bland.' He turned to Grace, 'She doesn't mean it. These are not her words.'

Grace's mother was lost in confusion. It was as if she could not even see her daughter.

Brittle laughter came from Mrs Bland. The crowd stirred.

'We both know you are a liar!' Skelton said to Mrs Bland. 'You have poisoned the truth, madam. You've controlled her mind.'

A tall man in the crowd brandished a heavy hammer in the air, waiting for one word from his leader. Others shouted in rage. People wanted to smash Skelton into splinters.

Grayling took his hand from his pocket. He was holding a gun.

'No!' Grace raged, seeing the gun. 'I will not let this happen!' She lifted her shield high, and stepped closer to Skelton. As she did this, the shield changed. Its reptile splotches flushed pure scarlet.

'On my command, Grayling,' said Mrs Bland.

Almost casually, Grayling took aim at Skelton.

'You really are an extraordinary girl,' said Skelton, ducking his head towards Grace. He was preparing to meet his end.

Extraordinary, thought Grace. I am Extra Ordinary. I am more than Ordinary. The facts had been there all the time. Why else would Mrs Bland hate me so much?

Grace laughed with untamed joy. The full force of her fury was arriving with an fiery feeling inside. She saw Mrs Bland, her enemy who wanted to kill her, and Grayling, his eyes narrowing as he took aim at Skelton. There was her mother, slack-faced and made stupid by the spell Mrs Bland had cast on her.

A long-sealed box in her heart sprang open, and out of it poured a wild red energy that surged in her legs and arms. Her fingers tingled with strength, her nails felt like the claws of a bear, her hair was as deadly as snakes, her limbs were as strong as oxen.

'I end this!' Grace sprang to her mother, seizing both her hands.

Mrs Brown's knees gave way. Grace tried to catch her elbows as she sank down.

'I love you, Grace!' Her Mother's voice was weak. 'I am so sorry...'

Grace had broken the spell and now, with fire in her eyes, she spun around to face her enemy. Mrs Bland was staring in amazement at Grayling's arm, which was frozen and trembling uncontrollably. 'I knew it, you little witch!' she said.

'Takes one to know one!' said Grace.

Sparkling with diamonds, Mrs Bland's fist lashed out.

Grace danced aside.

'Get away from her!' Grace's mother shouted at Mrs Bland, trying to get up from her knees. Grace realised that this was the voice of her real mother, the one she had been before all the grey madness.

The crowd shifted. For a second, they had a glimpse of Skelton and Grace as they truly were, as everyday people, not the monsters they were supposed to be.

With an immense effort Mrs Bland's iron willpower regained control.

Pain numbed Grace's legs. She dropped to her knees, whimpering. Skelton leant over to help.

Now the mind-controlled crowd could only see a skeleton man dressed in rags. His filthy claws groped at the shoulder of a rebellious girl, clutching a pathetic toy shield.

Proud and shining in the firelight, Mrs Bland loomed over Grace.

'What does your notebook say about bonfires?' She was speaking for the benefit of the television cameras. 'Nothing? Then let me enlighten you. In the old days a bonfire was pronounced *bone fire*.'

People in the crowd cheered.

'It is a fire to burn bones on!'

'*BURN THEM!*' roared the mob.

'Get away from us!' said Skelton, pointing his cutlass shakily towards Mrs Bland, who had taken a step closer.

The mob shifted. It was edging Skelton towards the flames.

Dancing to the fire's edge, Mrs Bland seized the end of a splintered chair leg, and pulled it from the living fire. She thrust it at Skelton. In her hands its flames changed, now they flared blue, orange and green.

'Why don't you climb in to the warm, Skelton?' she said using her beautiful voice, but her eyes were as hard as emeralds.

Suddenly, Skelton felt a dreadful urge to snuggle up in the warmth and comfort of a blanket of flames.

Resist her!

Don't sleep!

Never!

His mothers' voices sang in his head.

'We are woven together,' Skelton said with difficulty. 'Grace and I pulled your thread and you came to us, just as we wanted.'

'My, my!' said Mrs Bland. 'Just as *we* wanted?' She laughed derisively.

'Hear him!' Grace shouted, forcing the pain away. Now with a kind of exceptional concentration, she visualised Mrs Bland as powerless and begging for help.

Mrs Bland gasped. Weakened, she dropped the burning branch, and stumbled.

Again the crowd wavered.

'You! All of you! Wake up from this nightmare!' cried Skelton. 'Mrs Bland is no more Ordinary than I am, and nobody is more Normal than me. See her for what she is: a weaver of heartbreak for everyone. Ordinary and Normal.'

People were shouting in the crowd. Some had no idea why or how they were there. The people swayed; some stood blinking in confusion by the roaring bonfire.

Desperately, Mrs Bland again stabbed the burning wood at Skelton. His clothes caught fire. He dropped his cutlass. Frantically, he slapped at his chest as the greenish flames caught.

Mrs Bland rushed at him again, driving him towards the bone fire.

Grace threw herself forward. She struck her shield rim at the woman's forearm. Mrs Bland wheeled towards her now, wincing with pain. Grace had drawn blood.

'Why don't you leave everyone alone?' shouted Grace.

A madness gripped Skelton. His clothes still smouldering, teeth clenched nastily, he snatched up his cutlass and advanced on Mrs Bland. Even with a burnt hand clutching the Pin of Knots, he had murder in his heart.

'Grayling!' Mrs Bland shouted.

Still trembling wildly, Grayling fired a shot at Skelton. He missed. He shot again. The bullet whined past Skelton's head.

The Master of Yawngrave Tower swung his cutlass. In the next second, two fingers lay on the floor, and

Grayling's hand was gory with blood. But as Skelton stood there panting a thug darted behind him, and delivered a bone-crunching punch.

Skelton sprawled in the mud and ash. Two of his precious teeth slid across his tongue. His mouth bled.

Furiously, Grace sliced at the man with the edge of her shield. Something in its dragon hardness cleaved through the man's grey coat and cut him deeply.

The crowd had broken up. Some had fled, but a few stragglers remained, crazed with a desperate hatred. A woman ran at Skelton, stamping on his ribs as he tried to get off the ground.

'Delete them!' screamed Mrs Bland.

From nowhere a dark shape swooped towards the crowd.

'Hello Mother!'

Mrs Bland wailed in confusion for there, suddenly, was Rick, his wings spread wide.

'Hear him,' Grace ordered.

The remnants of the mob grew confused.

What was this? One of Mrs Bland's sons... Rick, wasn't it? With wings?

Skelton struggled to his feet, hardly able to breathe. He saw the bat boy land next to his mother. Would Rick betray them?

Chapter 31

The living grave

Rick had joined his mother!

Clutching the woven gold of the Pin of Knots in his burnt left fist and his cutlass in his right, defiantly and full of pain, Skelton spread his arms wide.

'Help me, Yawngrave Tower!' he cried. 'I am your Master!' His voice rang out clearly in the affray. Even Mrs Bland, staring at her son Rick, flinched.

A disturbing rumbling answered. The ground shook underfoot. Seconds later, an enormous root erupted from the trampled soil of the garden, and tore a line across the road. A great gush from a burst water main sprayed the fire. Steam hissed.

More roots ruptured the road surface. One, with the girth of an enormous tree trunk, looped around the parked digger and crushed it with incredible power. Others reared up from the ground, probing the air like giant tentacles. Many of the crowd ran, some screaming as they fled.

Rick sprang upwards into the air as a thin and sinuous wooden cobra rose up behind Mrs Bland. It struck, knocking her forwards. It whipped around her body, and dragged her to ground with a horrible force. Now it was more like a python than a cobra, binding her body in thick and crushing loops.

Grace stumbled through the confusion to where Mrs Bland was tied. With a thump, the bat boy landed next to her.

Casually, Rick folded his leathery wings and leant over a little to see his mother's face as she struggled. 'Hello again, Mother!' he said, squatting down as a subtle noose tightened around her neck.

With a terrible twisting hatred in her face, even now Mrs Bland tried to claw at her son's eyes. But Rick was beyond her reach. At last he was safe from her. He laughed heartlessly, until the tears rolled from his eyes. For his mother was being dragged into the earth, and nobody could stop it.

'See,' said Grace. 'You can't control *everything*. You might be able to control Rick, or these poor people, you might be able to control my parents... But you will never, ever control me!'

Grace's shield was still red with anger. More power surged through Grace that needed to escape. Needed vengeance! She raised her sharp-edged shield high over Mrs Bland's head...

'Stop! Grace, stop!'

Skelton's voice rose above the chaos. He was pointing directly at Grace. The order was for her; but it seemed to work for everyone.

Even the bitter remnants of the O.P.P. now scattered into the streets. Some threw off their grey clothing. Others wandered, dazed, into the surrounding streets, blinking in bewilderment. Many were hurt, lashed agonisingly by the roots of Yawngrave Tower.

Every single one of them was a victim of Mrs Bland's brainwashing hatred. Still, she writhed against her wooden bonds.

Reporters and TV crews were busy. Around the world Mrs Bland was trending on social media. For the world could at last see Mrs Bland for what she was. It had seen her Normal son, and witnessed her hypocrisy and violence.

Sirens wailed ever closer in the streets. For the first time in days, the police were coming, the fire service was coming, ambulances were coming. Flashing lights were being sent into the shadows Mrs Bland had cast.

Rick drank in the scene. Unflinchingly, and without any attempt to help, he watched his mother being stifled by the roots.

'Why are you laughing?' asked Grace.

There was no answer.

'Thank you, anyway,' said Grace. 'You helped us.'

'Whatever,' said Rick. He unfurled his wings. Without saying another word he flew up into the smoky sky and was gone.

Beneath Mrs Bland, the soil had loosened. Wooden ropes were now dragging her rapidly into the earth. Now only her face and neck still strained above the surface. She would be gone in seconds. People were running from all directions to bring help. It was too late.

'Sunny!' cried Skelton, rushing over. He fell on his knees. 'Sunny are you there?' For a second, he thought the green blaze had left her eyes, and she seemed puzzled. But the next moment, the green had returned. She stared at him with unmistakable venom.

'Don't think this is over, Yawngrave. Don't think that the hurly-burly's done. You must die, Skelton. If I die, you die. We are woven.'

Skelton backed away. 'Snake tongues! You lie,' he said.

Mrs Bland's eyes flicked onto Grace. 'As for you, you little witch. I prophesy this. You will never know...' The root tightened, squeezing the breath from her. 'Grace Brown,' she wheezed. 'Your life will be full of woe.'

Soil and mud bubbled up over the woman's face like boiling water. Grace and Skelton watched in horror as the light of Mrs Bland's eyes was extinguished. Her lips were the last to go, gasping one last lungful of air.

'Remember!' the lips said.

Skelton began retching, until he was violently sick. His body trembled from head to foot, his knees clicking.

Not knowing what to do, Grace patted his shoulder. But she was crying too.

Eventually Skelton collected himself, wiping his mouth with a red-and-gold-striped handkerchief.

'She's gone,' said Skelton, 'poor soul.'

'I hope so,' said Grace, trying not to imagine Mrs Bland being pulled through layers of mud and stone like a rag doll.

Chapter 32

When the hurly-burly's done

'I hope there are plenty of eatables in this victory celebration,' said Bonaparte.

'Use the evidence of your bulgy eyes, you wardrobe worrier,' said Skelton fondly.

Even Grace could see that the table had been spread with choice foods from the store- rooms of Yawngrave Tower. There was plenty of Ordinary food for her too, for she still found it hard to be tempted by Oaxacan fried grasshoppers, which Bonaparte claimed *put a spring in his step*, and made him *feel chirpy*.

Now there was time, everyone began to explore the Tower. They peered into the entrance of the cupboard under the stairs. But if there had been any bomb damage, it had already healed. Chiefly what they found in the upper floors were honeycombs of little rooms and chambers, all smelling of green wood. Some were no larger than small cupboards, others the size of Grace's bedroom at home, others far taller than they were wide.

In one they found rings of mushrooms, which Grace identified (now that they had the internet again) as Fairy Ring Champignons and common field mushrooms.

Bonaparte immediately went downstairs, saying they would be delicious and everyone could eat them. Spoony disagreed of course, as he did not eat at all. As they trooped into the kitchen, there was a brisk tapping of the bat-faced knocker on the front door.

Skelton groaned.

'What a week. Probably another film crew,' he said cheerfully, turning to Grace. 'Shall we?'

'*Someone* is enjoying all this attention far too much for his own good' Fibula said.

'That was a bit catty,' said Grimsby.

But the truth was that even Skelton's jaws ached after days of uninterrupted talking. While Grace tried to avoid speaking to anyone. This, however, only increased people's curiosity. Against her will, she was having a moment of celebrity too.

What was annoying was that however clearly Skelton and Grace told their story, every reporter wanted to invent something to add to it.

One article called Skelton, *Shelton Yorngrave* throughout the piece. Someone in America had written a blog post 'proving' that Grace was really an alien from another planet, and that Mrs Bland had never really existed. Quite a few people said that Grace was 'confused' or that she had been born Normal but had been given away to Ordinary parents. Of all the rumours, this last one upset Grace most.

It had been five days since the bone fire night battle, and still her parents had still not come to see her. It was rumoured that the police had been interviewing them, and that they had been hounded by news reporters. In contrast, the parents of Hortense, Victor and Viking had come the morning after Mrs Bland had been overthrown, having been immediately released from Mrs Bland's 'hospitality'. Their gratitude for Skelton's protection of their children, who had slept soundly throughout the battle, was so great that Skelton felt embarrassed.

Old habits die hard. When Grace and Skelton reached the front door, Skelton squinted through the O-shaped mouth of his fish-faced spy hole. Outside he saw an Ordinary man and woman. The woman was carrying a spare coat.

Without a word, he unchained the door, which opened to a little symphony of creaks and complaints.

Grace stared, but did not speak.

'Mr and Mrs Brown. It's a pleasure to meet you again,' Skelton said very politely.

'That's right,' said Mr Brown, nervously.

Grace still said nothing.

'Aren't you going to speak to your parents?' asked Skelton, concerned.

Grace took a hesitant step towards them. Her mother made a strange sound: a great sobbing gulp. Huge tears began to run down her cheeks.

'Mum!' said Grace, and she ran into her mother's arms. Her real mother, not the mind-controlled automaton Mrs Bland had made of her. Just her own true mother.

Grace's mother held her fiercely, and they both sobbed and kissed each other's faces. Next, Grace's father was wrapping them both in his arms and he cried too.

'We're sorry,' he said. 'So terribly sorry. We're back to our usual selves now.'

'Your daughter is an excellent girl,' Skelton said, wiping his eyes with a spotted handkerchief.

'We know that,' said Mr Brown.

'Would you like to join us for some supper?' said Bonaparte, emerging from the kitchen wearing an apron. 'We have mushrooms, and were about to have a feast to celebrate better times. We have lots of Ordinary food, haven't we, Grace?'

By now all the inhabitants of Yawngrave Tower had come to the front door, curious to see Grace's parents.

'That is a very kind offer, Mr Yawngrave,' said Mrs Brown, trying not to look at Spoony Kooker. I'm afraid I want to be selfish. I want Grace all to myself. We have been kept apart for so long, I just need her to be at home with me.'

'Of course,' said Bonaparte. 'I completely understand.'

There was an awkward pause.

'Say it Skelton,' said Fibula.

'Ah yes. There is another thing we all want to… Um – '

'The thing is,' said Bonaparte, 'that we have a gift for you. As you would expect, it is a very Normal gift.'

Grace did not know what to say.

'We would, all of us that is…' Skelton cleared his throat. 'We would like to give you a name to add to your collection. From this moment you are not just "Grace Brown" to us. You are Magnificent Grace Brown. We hope you like it.' The others murmured in agreement.

'It's one of the best presents I've ever had,' Grace said. 'I shall treasure it.'

'You are always welcome here, Magnificent Grace Brown,' Skelton said. For some reason he was staring at his shiny shoes as he said this. Grace ran back to kiss Skelton and Bonaparte, and reach up to Spoony, who floated gravely above. Grace imagined she felt a slight, foggy coolness at his touch. There was a warm goodbye with Fibula with plenty of hugs, and Grimsby too. She even dared to rumple the Old General between the ears, an act of affection Tibia permitted with half-closed eyes.

'This house is your house, my dear,' said Fibula. 'Come back tomorrow,' she added.

'And the day after that,' said Tibia.

Mr and Mrs Brown laughed a little uncomfortably, but kept smiling.

Grace took her parents' hands, her mother on one side, her father on the other. As they reached the pavement, and Grace turned back to see Skelton hold up his Pin of Knots, and Grace saw that everyone was looking happy and sad at the same time. Then the door closed, with a resonant clang.

'Thank goodness, that's over,' said Mrs Brown, smoothing a speck of something from her coat. 'Let's go home, Grace. There are so many things I want to tell you.'

They hurried along Skelton's street, which was still being repaired from the damage it had taken. In ten minutes they would be home.

'Where's Molly?' asked Grace.

'She's at home. Next door is keeping an eye on her. Your sister can't wait to see you.'

'I can't wait to see her either,' said Grace happily.

'Well, said Bonaparte, 'those mushrooms won't eat themselves, will they?'

The thought of food made everyone feel happier as they hurried towards the kitchen.

'Oh, look Skelton! She's forgotten it,' said Bonaparte stopping for a moment, by the cupboard under the stairs. Propped against the round door was Grace's shield.

'We'll keep it safe for her,' Skelton said.

Chapter 33

The Golden Cockerel

Even without Grace, there was still an excellent party to be had in the War Room.

'We're all too serious,' said Fibula almost as soon as they had climbed upstairs. 'I think it is time to get girlsterous.'

'Girlsterous isn't a word,' said Bonaparte.

'I say it is. It is like being boisterous but better. Put some music on, Skelton!' Soon she was doing a spidery kind of dancing, her blue eyes gleeful in her furry face. Before long everyone else was leaping and cavorting too.

'Now for the bucket game,' Skelton said, when they had all tired of dancing. Skelton produced a brass bucket. With an elegant low bow, he handed it to Bonaparte who, after removing one of his dressier party monocles, plunged in his head and began to laugh. His mirth echoed louder and louder before spilling out to infect everyone else with the giggles. Next came Tibia, whose bloodcurdling screech of a laugh had Fibula rolling on the floor with her six legs waggling. One by one, everyone had a turn, especially Spoony Kooker who insisted on several. They spent lots of time arguing happily among themselves who had the funniest laugh.

Eventually, Skelton slipped away from the group to stand on a fine balcony that had only recently begun to bulge out from the side of the Tower. For a moment, he enjoyed the sight of a little boat being rowed down the river.

He sighed. In a few days, Mrs Bland's grip on Ordinary people would begin to seem like a bad dream. Already the Siege of Yawngrave Tower and the Bone Fire Night battle had become old stories. No journalists had contacted him for two days. No longer did any camera crews wait outside in the street hoping to catch a glimpse of him. Fewer people each day seemed interested in what he had to say about the danger of Mrs Bland's kind of thinking. Ordinary people's memories are short.

Tibia jumped up onto the ledge Skelton was leaning on. He had little fear of heights.

Together, they squinted companionably into the November sunset. Although it was a cool day, the light was unusually golden.

'One of the terrible things about fighting,' said Tibia, is that it makes people unhappy for a long time afterwards too. I hope peace has come to stay this time. We should try to enjoy today, Skelton, for no one can say what will happen tomorrow.'

In answer, Skelton scratched a fleabite behind the old soldier's ear as they surveyed the ruined front garden. Below them, men were busy with heavy machinery, and were repairing the road from the effects of the bone fire and the weird roots of Yawngrave Tower. Skelton's fence would be rebuilt too.

'Is something still troubling you Skelton?' asked Tibia.

'I keep wondering how my lovely childhood friend Sunny Applebiter Dolmalus could have grown up to become Mrs Bland. I remember that she was bullied at school. It was horrible for her, but it is the sort of thing that can happen to anyone...'

Tibia furrowed his head.

'And,' Skelton continued, 'I can understand why her life was woven in with mine, because we grew up in this very street, and went to the same school. My noble father was very fond of Sunny too. What I don't understand is why Grace was woven into this battle? It troubles me that Grace reminded me of Sunny, but I can't say why.'

'She's an extraordinary person, and so it seems was Sunny. Let's hope Grace doesn't end up the same way,' said Tibia.

'That couldn't happen, could it?' Skelton sounded anxious. 'We must keep an eye on her.'

Behind them was a soft jingling of bells.

Tibia spun round with his back arched. Suddenly his rumpled old features broke into an expression of joy.

How long the Golden Cockerel had been on the balcony, listening to their conversation, Tibia did not know. He found himself in the presence of the most beautiful creature he had ever seen. And now Skelton saw it too.

It was the Golden Cockerel in all its glory. Its body reflected scintillations of soft sunset light. Its eyes were unfathomable pools of mercury.

'*Well done*,' said the Golden Cockerel in its strange fluting voice.

'Pardon?' Skelton blurted out.

'*Well done*,' it said again.

'Thank you,' said Tibia.

'Thank you. Yes, thank you, O Golden Cockerel,' Skelton said, bowing. 'You are very welcome indeed to Yawngrave Tower. This is Tibia, and my name is—'

'*I sit in the tree*,' said the Golden Cockerel.

Skelton was not quite sure what the Golden Cockerel had meant. The noble way it spoke, however, made him feel it was communicating something extremely important. Skelton also felt that the wonderous being was saying that Yawngrave Tower, which was by now very treelike indeed, was even more important than the Golden Cockerel itself. Not that any of this was said in actual words.

'*The tree will return to itself,*' said the Golden Cockerel.

Instantly, and without warning, the corners of the ornate balcony began to shrink. Skelton backed away from the melting edge, towards the doorway of the War Room.

Both Tibia and Skelton understood what it meant: Yawngrave Tower must decline. It must become an everyday Normal house in an everyday street, and it was starting now.

Skelton felt sad.

'O Golden Cockerel,' said Tibia gruffly, 'does this mean the danger is over?'

'*The tree is always in danger,*' it piped. Gracefully, with a faint whirr, it hopped onto the edge of the softening balcony which sank a little under its weight.

The miraculous bird was so close they could have touched it. Of course, because this would have been disrespectful, they did not.

The Golden Cockerel flew. How this was possible, Skelton could not say. All that gold seemed far too heavy. Nevertheless it climbed into the sky and flew west towards the sunset.

To get a last look, Tibia and Skelton again leant dangerously on the edge of the balcony, that was now dripping like candle wax, to catch a final glint of gold in the sunset. Above them, the crown of treelike towers were already telescoping down into themselves, their spiral staircases coiling like tight springs.

Chapter 34

The Warden's return

'The Cockerel!' said Tibia, as they stepped back into the party.

'We saw it and it was beautiful,' Skelton added dreamily.

Fibula, Spoony, Bonaparte and Grimsby had been too busy enjoying themselves, to notice the walls inching inwards. But now everyone could see cabinets of weapons folding back into themselves, and doors to storerooms and chambers softly sealing up. In fact, the entire War Room was now shrinking rapidly, and growing darker as, one by one, candles were reabsorbed into the walls.

'We need to go downstairs,' said Skelton. 'Sadly, as you can see, Yawngrave Tower is becoming a house again.

They walked down the quickly dwindling stairs to the Long Room. Stepping into it Skelton noticed again the bare patches on the walls, where the portraits of his ancestors had been.

Spoony drifted in, to hover over the Long Room's long table.

'My friends,' said Spoony. 'I have to go now.'

'But we're in the middle of the party, you can't go!' said Bonaparte.

'Don't be a party pooper Spoony Kooker,' said Grimsby.

'I don't want to make a fuss, and I hate goodbyes,' said Spoony. 'I will miss you all, but I must be upstairs now the darkness is forming again. I am the guardian of the Yawngrave ancestors, and I have my duty to perform.'

'You have done your duty with honour,' Skelton's face was serious, 'and yet you have paid the highest price for your loyalty.'

Everyone cheered Spoony. He folded in a strange courtly bow.

'Goodbye!' said Spoony. Before anyone could say more, he flashed away.

'My portraits!' Skelton yelped. He hurried after the retreating ghoul, but found Spoony waiting to speak to him.

'Skelton,' he said. 'You understand, don't you?'

'Yes,' Skelton said. 'You are the faithful spirit of Yawngrave Tower, and you want to resume your duty.

Besides, the Golden Cockerel said "the tree will return to itself" and that's why the house is doing just that.'

They listened to the Tower adjusting all around them.

Skelton followed Spoony. There were no longer stairs up to the War Room. Instead they stood under the trapdoor opening into the attic. Spoony simply melted through the trapdoor without opening it. Skelton, however, had to climb onto a chair, and haul himself up until he found his head poking once more into a vague and empty space.

'Here you are,' said Spoony, indicating the paintings of Skelton's father and grandfather, which were exactly where Bonaparte had left them. The ghost had begun to emit a faint light, and by this Skelton could see that his ancestor's faces remained as handsome as ever.

'Spoony Pootus Olly Osgood Kooker, Warden of Yawngrave Tower, guardian of my ancestors,' Skelton said formally. 'I thank you for all your services and courage.'

'Thank you, Skelton Kirkley Elvis Lionel Lupus Yawngrave III. Your ancestors will be proud of you.'

Skelton turned back to the trapdoor. Below him was his life and his friends. Perhaps it was the thought of so many ancestors overhead, however, that tugged at his bones. But Spoony Kooker was watching him carefully.

'Not yet, Skelton,' said Spoony.

'See you later then,' said Skelton.

'Not too soon, I hope,' said Spoony with a long laugh that echoed in the second kind of darkness.

Downstairs they were dancing again.

Chapter 35

The thread

'That was a visit I won't forget,' Bonaparte said as he packed his suitcase. Skelton was watching every move, for already he had rescued one of his favourite ties, and his third-best monocle from Bonaparte's case.

'Something still bothers me, though,' said Bonaparte, folding a pair of stripy trousers. 'Grace's mother and father. I know they were perfectly polite to us, but I still don't trust them.'

'Why?' said Skelton.

'Let me see...' said Bonaparte thoughtfully. 'Maybe it's because Mr Brown tried to strangle me in a rib restaurant. Call me old-fashioned, Skelton, but I don't like that sort of thing. Seeing them collect Grace gave me a funny feeling, and not "ha-ha" funny, more of a "hmmmmm" funny.'

'Really? "Hmmmm funny", you say?' Skelton repeated thoughtfully.

'And although I saw Mrs Bland being dragged underground with my own eyes, I don't think her kind of evil is over,' Skelton said.

Bonaparte screwed a monocle (one of his own) into his eye socket.

'It never is,' he said. 'But for now, be happy, Skelly.'

Together they dragged Bonaparte's case to the front door.

'This is seems heavier than I remember it,' said Skelton suspiciously.

'Oh,' said Bonaparte airily, 'I popped in a few jars from the storeroom before it folded away. Anyway… Must go! Taxi's here.'

Skelton waved him off, and Tibia, Fibula and Grimsby joined him at the doorstep.

'Take care, you old creaker,' called Fibula.

'Cheerio, Boney!' called Tibia.

'You too, you weasels,' said Bonaparte. 'And you, Grimsby.' Here Bonaparte winked at the Normal dog. 'See you soon.'

After Skelton closed the door, Grimsby began shifting from one paw to another, with an awkward smile on his face.

'What's this?' asked Skelton.

'Our comrade Grimsby needs a home,' said Tibia.

Some time later, Grimsby and his new feline housemates had curled up in the kitchen after a light snack. Grimsby was snoring loudly.

Skelton began to pace about his home, as if to reacquaint himself with it. He had come to realise that the Tower did not belong to him. It was the other way round. He belonged to the Tower, and the Tower was connected to the world in ways he did not understand.

He entered the Long Room, and stood in the presence of the portraits of his father and grandfather, now back in their rightful places. The embers of a fire were still glowing in the grate, *A miniature bone fire*, he thought with a shudder.

Time for bed. His joints were stiff with the approaching winter, and he creaked upstairs to his bedroom. Soon he was dangling comfortably from his bed hooks, listening to his grandfather clock.

Tut-tut-tut.

At last, Skelton Yawngrave's home was a place of peace again.

Tut-tut-tut.

Before he slept, Skelton held the triangles of woven gold that his mothers and father had given him.

Tut-tut-tut...

He dreamt of Mrs Bland. She appeared to him still struggling, green-eyed under the earth. Skelton woke trembling. His own shout had woken him up. Even in the other world of sleep, even though Mrs Bland was dead, it seemed there was a thread that wove them together.

Chapter 36

Home is where the heart is

'All I want, Grace, is for everything to be exactly as it was before all the trouble with Normals started,' said her mother after they had eaten their very Ordinary dinner. 'I just want you to be happy.'

Molly, who had been over-excited for most of the day, was fast asleep on the sofa next to Grace. She had not left her sister's side since she returned.

'Thanks, Mum,' said Grace.

'We understand that you might not want to talk about everything just yet,' said Mrs Brown. 'You've had a terrible ordeal. That's right isn't it, Bob?'

'Yes,' said Mr Brown. 'She probably needs to go to sleep now, like her sister.'

Grace was troubled.

'On the internet they said you adopted me,' she said. 'That I'm not your real daughter, that I don't really belong to you.'

'Oh darling,' said Mr Brown. 'That's crazy. Of course you're our real daughter. Look! You have my eyes, don't you? And your mother's hair?'

'I suppose so,' said Grace.

'Come on, Grace,' said her mother. 'You obviously need a good sleep, in your own bed. You've kept some funny company lately, it will be good for you to feel safe and secure.'

Her parents hugged and kissed her.

'All I want,' said Grace's mother again, 'is for everything be exactly as it was before. Now, have a good night darling.'

Later, wide-eyed in her own bed, Grace's mind was still working. *I'm different now*, she thought. She remembered how pure the feeling of her own mysterious power had been when she was fighting against Mrs Bland. What was right, and what was wrong, seemed clearer when her arch enemy was alive.

Now she had to fit back into Ordinary life, and pretend to be an Ordinary girl. But she wasn't Ordinary, was she? She was *extraordinary*. She was Magnificent Grace Brown. So if these people really were her parents, there would have to be some changes. There would have to be... To be…

At last, merciful sleep stole over Grace.

Elsewhere, two people in our story were still awake.

Spoony Kooker was guarding the doorway of a room that opened into endless time. Inside were the bones of the sleeping Yawngraves, and Yarpgraters, Yawngraefs and others. He did it with neither sadness nor joy. One day Skelton Kirkley Elvis Lionel Lupus Yawngrave III would settle his old bones in the Red Room. He would fall into the long dreamless bliss among his forefathers. Spoony would be there for him.

Hanging in the unreachable dark, Spoony felt happy at last. For he finally had time to treasure the memory of Diana Yellyface.

For what was a holiday downstairs compared to the slow ebbing of decades in which he could be alone with his thoughts?

His imagination, overstimulated by recent events, had not quite settled. It was playing tricks. It filled the air with half-glimpsed objects.

One, a tiny mote of silver dust fainter than a firefly, weaved towards him through the second kind of darkness.

It was the ghost of a death's-head hawkmoth.

'Hello. Spoony,' said Diana Yellyface.

As Grace slept quietly in her own bed, another person was still awake.

Above the ceiling of her room was a loft space where the Browns had stored old suitcases, broken lamps, boxes of things that they could never decide whether to throw out or keep.

Above the loft was the tiled roof. Tonight the tiles were greasy with drizzle and damp; dead November leaves stuck to them.

Still as a gargoyle, Rick crouched by the chimney. He had spied Grace entering the house with her parents and laughed sourly. It seemed everybody, except for him, could return to their everyday lives as if nothing had happened. He watched the streams of traffic, the people walking home on the streets, the trains rattling across the bridge. Up here on the roof, hunched in the rain, he was free to fly where he wanted. But where that was, exactly, he could not decide.

He became aware of his arm. Quite suddenly it had begun tingling. With a horrific sense of recognition, he watched his arm jut out in front of him, and his mind... His mind...

Without warning his body toppled forward, slithering down the sloping roof towards the front of the house. Wings still furled, he hung on the gutter, facing the curtained window of Grace's bedroom.

A green fire was burning in his eyes.

THE END

<u>Your disobedience has been noted</u>

If you have read this copy of *Magnificent Grace*
without permission, you will be punished.

Events in the book suggest that the Ordinary
People's Party had been defeated, and that I, Mrs
Bland, have been assassinated by terrorists. This is
fake news. This book is a fiction, nothing more than a
silly story. The Ordinary People's Party is alive and
well.

And of course, as its leader, so am I.

Magnificent Grace is not the only book of this type.
Rumours suggest a sequel is being prepared. It is
thought copies of this will soon begin circulating
illegally. If you see one please delete it or hand it in
for burning at once.

Ordinary is as Ordinary does!

Ann Bland
Chief Executive and Chairperson
Ordinary People's Party

Skelton Kirkley Elvis Lionel Lupus Yawngrave III thanks children in Brighton and West Sussex schools who listened to early versions of this story and gave him insightful and inspiring feedback.

Skelton would also like to thank:

Calliope the cat who listened to the story as it was written
Charlotte Norman for invaluable editorial help
Dawn Daniel an outstanding teacher who has helped him reach out to readers
Ellie Francesca Watson for the cover painting of Grace
Margaret Hamlin for artistic stimulus, including Skelton's back cover portrait, and talkative cliff walks
Rosie Taylor for brainy and inspirational advice on children's books.

Lorraine Kenny last, but far from least, for her love, wise guidance and splendid piemaking.

For more about The Witch Grace Brown Adventures visit
www.skeltonyawngrave.com